IN SEARCH OF
THE VIKINGS

A Cumbrae Crime Novel

Margaret MacGregor

belnahuabooks

ISBN-978-1-9168701-1-6

Cover design by: Margaret MacGregor

To my parents, grandparents and twin sisters who inculcated a love of Cumbrae in long happy summer holidays in the family room and kitchen and to my uncle who bought me my first camera and took so many excellent family photos.

It was not man's power which drove him away, but the power of God which crushed his ships and sent a pestilence among his troops. Such of them as mustered to engage on the third day of Michaelmas, God defeated and slew by the footmen of the country. Thus they were compelled to carry off their wounded and slain to their ships, and to return home in more disgraceful plight than they had left it.

MELROSE CHRONICLE

CONTENTS

PREFACE

When a young team of students start on an archaeological dig, they hope to find evidence of the Vikings on the Scottish Isle of Cumbrae. They do not expect to find a body of a young girl who vanished thirty years before, as well as a hoard of Viking treasure. Is it too late to solve the mystery of her death and find the perpetrator? The lives and loves of young people in modern day Scotland are blended with the fate of a royal rebel, a Norse princess, who refuses to accept a traditional role in thirteenth century Norway and chooses a husband and a life of her own far from her native land.

A Scottish historical novel based on the Battle of Largs, fought in 1263 to settle whether Scotland or Norway ruled the Western Isles.

Share the tension as the story builds to a dramatic conclusion which could end in tragedy.

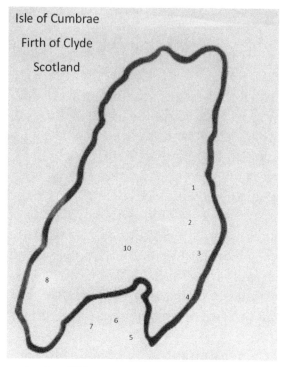

Isle of Cumbrae

Firth of Clyde

Scotland

1.	Largs/Millport Ferry	6.	Crocodile Rock
2.	Haakon's Mound	7.	West Bay
3.	Dig Site	8.	Fintry Bay
4.	Hostel	9.	Cathedral of the Isles
5.	Kames Bay	10.	Glaid Stone

BATTLE OF LARGS 1263

No-one knew where King Haakon of Norway would land on the mainland of Scotland to battle it out with the Scots for the right to rule the Western Isles.

CUMBRAE 2005

Alice McGlynn grasped the bag from the luggage carousel and hoisted it onto her back. She was wearing too many clothes for the mild September weather, but one way of coping with budget airline restrictions was to wear your luggage rather than to pack it. Once she was on the train to Largs she could shed a few layers and stuff them into her backpack.

The bus to Glasgow was waiting right outside the terminal at Glasgow Airport and in less than half an hour she was in the concourse of Glasgow Central Station under the tracery of Victorian glass and ironwork, clutching a coffee to take on the next stage of her journey to the Isle of Cumbrae.

"Where?" her friends at Trinity College Dublin had asked, when they heard she was applying for a place on this inter-university archaeological dig. Back home in Ireland folk tended to have heard of only a few Scottish islands; Skye was high up on the list; the whisky aficionados dreamt of the distillery trail on Islay; Jura was the destination of the huntin' shootin' and fishin' breed, who could afford to live in regency town houses in the Georgian neighbourhood of Dublin. But generally, the Isle of Cumbrae, fewer than forty miles from Glasgow, was a gem little known outside the west of Scotland.

As the train sped through agricultural land that was not so very different from her native Ireland, Alice wished she had been able to arrive at the same time as the rest of the group. The dig was not due to start till tomorrow but the accommodation had been available since the day before and she would have preferred to have had a period to settle in, get to know the place and, even more important, to meet the other students who had gained a place on this course. Alice was an attractive girl, popular with her peers, but in new social situations she lacked confidence. This was a novel venture for her and she hoped she'd be able to integrate easily.

It was a set-back that she had to be late. Her university tutor had not been able to schedule their meeting till yesterday, so she would be arriving at the tail end, when everyone else had been able to get together as a group. She hated the thought that she would be the odd one out.

Not for the first time she wondered what this project would be like. The advertisement on the university notice board had been intriguing, but left plenty of questions unanswered. The course application form had some decidedly odd features.

"Do you ride a bicycle?"

"What on earth has that to do with whether you're suitable to help with a medieval archaeological project?" her friends asked. "Maybe it's to check your green credentials," her friend Maura suggested. There was no obvious answer, however, and she dismissed it from her mind. Participation in the course counted as a credit and would look good on her application form, when she came to apply for entry to the Masters course.

The train drew up at Largs station, the terminal on the line, only a few hundred yards from the Firth of Clyde. When she left the station Alice found herself in a street of small shops and cafes that led straight down to the harbour, where the Cumbrae ferry was already drawing into the pier. Alice shouldered her rucksack and headed for the ticket office. Once loaded with whatever foot passengers and vehicles were waiting, the ferry set off across the firth.

From the rail of the upper deck she saw the island of Great Cumbrae for the first time and briefly, off to the south, the smaller island of Little Cumbrae, although this disappeared

4

from view as the ship neared the landing stage. The journey took only ten minutes but Alice enjoyed the view westward to the low-lying island that was to be home for the next ten days.

Vehicles were allowed to disembark before the pedestrians, but, only one lorry and two cars made the journey, and, less an hour after she had arrived in Largs, Alice was making her way up the short slipway towards the main road round Cumbrae.

The lorry and cars turned right and disappeared round the coastal road. A bus waited at the stop to take the foot passengers into Millport, the only town on the island. As Alice headed for it, she was approached by a young man, who had been leaning on the rail opposite the bus stop.

"Are you by any chance, Alice McGlynn?" His friendly gaze took in her laden rucksack, as she nodded in answer. "I'm Dean Redcliff. Prof Hughes asked me to meet you. We more or less knew when you'd be likely to arrive. Can I help you with that?"

"No need," Alice bridled at the suggestion. "I've managed fine so far."

A mistake, thought Dean; she was one of the tetchy ones. It was such a minefield nowadays. Open a door or give way to a female and you could be pounced on as a patronising supporter of male superiority. "Sorry," he grinned. "Blame my mother. She brought me up badly. With great difficulty, I've been able to wean myself off calling females ladies and standing up when one enters a room. Knights Errant Anonymous has helped. But I still backslide. Actually I just wanted to persuade you to put your rucksack on the bus and to dissuade you from accompanying it. I've got your bike here. The dig and the hostel are this way. The bus is going that way." He gestured to left and right. "It will get to the hostel eventually and Jimmy will drop your rucksack off then. That's what the Prof has arranged."

Alice shrugged the rucksack from her back and smiled at him. "Thanks." She handed her gear to Jimmy and watched as the bus set off on its anti-clockwise journey round the island.

"You're starting to get acclimatised quickly," Dean remarked. "Watching the bus is one of the major excitements on this island. A ship at Keppel Pier attracts a crowd. If the Waverley paddle steamer arrives it counts as a major event. Right now we'll go straight to the hostel, but we pass the dig on the way. We haven't started work yet; the others are at the site now but just for a preliminary look round so you haven't missed anything. We can give them a quick wave but the Prof says you might want to see your room and settle in. After that we can see if there's time to go back before supper. The first briefing is at eight tonight. The schedule is pretty packed, you'll find."

Together they wheeled their bicycles to the main road.

"There aren't many travel decisions to be made; clockwise or anti-clockwise, all roads lead to Millport. Normally the bus goes clockwise to Millport as it's the shorter way, but sections of that route are closed for roadworks. We have permission to go through by bike, as we need access. You'll get the picture as we go." He swung onto the road and led the way.

Small rocky beaches fringed the coast road. As they cycled on Alice found the views attractive, and this included the sight of Dean as he peddled steadily in front, his broad muscular shoulders bent over the handlebars. She knew she had been rather curmudgeonly about the rucksack, but he hadn't taken umbrage and she liked his sense of humour. A *definite maybe* as a friend, she decided.

Fewer than two miles further on she saw the excavation site, obvious from the marquees that had been pitched to provide shelter. Posts had been hammered in to hold the surrounding tape that marked the extent of the dig; some figures dotted the scene. Dean rang a peal on his bicycle bell, sat back in the saddle and waved, but didn't slow his pace. The figures glanced round and some waved, but Alice had no time to return their greetings before she was past the site and peddling faster to catch up.

Soon she saw Dean turn right, and head into the grounds of a group of buildings. The first building was modern, a two storey structure; the other was an older sandstone building.

Dean dismounted and led the way into the hostel. "I'll let Mrs Macbeth take over now." He gestured to a door on the right. "This is our common room. It has an urn and we can help ourselves to tea and coffee any time. "I'll either be there or in the research room till supper." A woman appeared and he continued, "This is Alice, Mrs Macbeth. Jimmy is bringing her luggage round." He smiled at them. "See you later, ladies." With a provocative grin at Alice he headed off down the corridor.

Upstairs Mrs Macbeth opened the door to Alice's room. Your card just needs to be swiped at the door lock. It will also get you in the main door. Some of the other rooms, the common room and the library, have an entry pad. You'll find the details in the folder on your desk. I've put the three lasses on this floor and the lads down below. It's not Scottish Calvinist prudishness. It's just favouritism. There's a better view and a separate sitting room with TV and so on, in case anyone needs a bit of peace and quiet. The bedrooms don't have TVs. This is a hostel, not a hotel. You'll find all the times for meals in your folder, but supper tonight is at six. Would you like something to eat just now? If you've been travelling on some budget airline or other, you probably haven't had much food."

"No thanks, Mrs Macbeth. I'm sure I can last out till then."

"Right. When Jimmy comes with your things I'll give you a shout. I'll leave you to settle in now."

◆ ◆ ◆

Alice settled comfortably into the sofa beside her new friend, Graziella, a vivacious student from Padua, while Professor Alan Hughes held the floor later that evening for the first official briefing of the course.

"Welcome to the Greater Cumbrae Archaeological Project." He had an easy manner and he and Dr O'Flaherty, were set to perform a confident double-act in their introductory session. The audience of ten students seemed a promising lot, so far, from various universities across Europe.

"You have all been chosen, after a rigorous selection process, to take part in this prestigious international inter-varsity event, made possible only through generous funding secured by Dr O'Flaherty here, whose 'good-natured buffoon' act disguises a ruthless calculating man who will stoop to any chicanery to achieve his ends."

"Sure, it's just learning to use the right words. *'The students will learn to work as a team'* blah, blah, blah." O'Flaherty grinned wolfishly at the group. "I could run a master class on how to write successful funding bids. Make a fortune I would. *Shibboleths and Other Shy – ah - Slogans: terminology to impress grant committees.*"

"Meanwhile," Alan continued, "you have him to thank for your luxurious accommodation at the University Marine Biological Station, conveniently situated mid-way between our dig site and the busy metropolis of Millport, the main, indeed the only, town on the island."

His audience chuckled obediently. Those who had arrived early had already reconnoitred the handful of streets that made up the small seaside resort. The only businesses were strung along one side of the esplanade facing the beach, some cafes, pubs and smaller shops catering to the visitors in search of gifts, or spades and pails for the children.

"Your day will be very full, but only some of it will be digging with trowels. This is still the most important activity in field archaeology, but it can be back-breaking work. Folk speak disparagingly of Health and Safety but there's no long-term advantage in ignoring the need for a change of position and activity. There'll be an opportunity to learn a variety of key archaeological skills. Your part is to turn up on time at the specified venues on your schedule, the main dig site, the town library and museum, where we have reserved a research room..."

"And *The Crocodile Rock* pub where we have reserved a snug room and negotiated group rates for the beer," interrupted O'Flaherty.

"Anyone stupid enough to try to get discounted beer from

Martin McCrone will soon learn the hard way to put no trust in Dr O'Flaherty's word." Hughes was the straight man in the double act, a foil to O'Flaherty's clowning. "To continue, we have also provided a fleet of bicycles for general use, although I see a couple of you have brought your own. These are your responsibility. For the rest there is only one proviso, that they aren't left overnight at the dig site, or in the town. If you decide that it's safer to walk back from the pub, then wheel the bike with you."

"And park responsibly," O'Flaherty added. "If you see a sign on any windows, *Nae Bikes,* take it very seriously. Believe me you don't want to tangle with any of the fierce hairy locals. And the men are almost as bad."

"All the housekeeping arrangements are in the folder in your room. Mrs Macbeth and her team will provide you with breakfast, packed lunch and dinner. If you don't intend to turn up for the evening meal let her know. And, by the way, she's heard all the Shakespeare jokes, so don't irritate her. Christopher Marlowe, Berthold Brecht and Alexander McCall Smith are her authors of choice."

At the coffee break, Dean helped himself to a shortbread biscuit and made his way towards Alice and Graziella. "So you got settled in all right?" As a chat-up line it was hardly inspired, but it would do. "How did the meeting go? Good feedback on your progress?"

"Yes, thank goodness. Now I can relax and concentrate on becoming a second Amelia Peabody." Dean raised a quizzical eyebrow. He'd been practising in front of the mirror and judged that now was the time to try out the mannerism publicly. He hoped it would bolster his Byronic man-of-the-world image.

"She's a fictional Victorian archaeologist and detective, making her mark in a male-dominated field."

"Ah," Dean was stymied. He did not want to venture into the dangerous territory of gender equality, or swap book club choices. Uncertain what to say next, he held out the plate. "Would you like a biscuit?"

Across the room, Paul Aitken had homed in on the third female in the group, Kathryn Thomas, a statuesque blonde from Aberystwyth, who held her coffee mug as if it were a champagne glass.

"I see you brought your own bike too. I've brought my San Remo. Maybe we could take a spin together. Have you had the Hellcat long? She's a beauty."

"Mm," Kathryn's reply was non-committal. She was keeping her options open, as she eyed the rest of the group. Apart from Paul and Dean there were five other males, two so uncannily alike that it was obvious that they were twins. She turned her attention back to Paul, who was obviously trying to impress.

"I do long-distance. Do you race?"

"Oh just tooling around the village at home." Paul was too experienced to be caught in an easy lie. "Not much long-distance cycling here, even if half of the road wasn't under repair. "But there are some lovely bijou bays and beaches. We could lunch and admire the scenery."

"Mm, maybe," Kathryn drifted off.

O'Flaherty had looked round the students speculatively before gravitating towards Paul. He had noticed the impressive address when glancing through the application forms. It was always worth cultivating potential donors. Universities now had to seek funding where they could, and successes increased your likelihood of being recommended for government quangos and advisory boards. But he decided to leave it to a more opportune moment. Kathryn's rebuff was obvious and Paul had been left looking decidedly chagrined, before shrugging ruefully.

As O'Flaherty rattled a spoon against a mug to signal the end of the break, Paul headed for an armchair and took his seat undaunted, resolved to consider the putdown as a challenge.

"Just a few background notes, before we stop this session." Alan Hughes once again led the briefing. "On Cumbrae it doesn't matter if the road is closed at any point. You can always go round the island the other way. It might take you longer to reach your destination but, since the total circumference is a mere eleven miles, most people accept the detour philosophically.

"Work on the road is a boon to archaeologists. Only during that limited time, while the road surface is bulldozed before being replaced, is it possible to probe further into a burial ground, that was discovered in 1873. It's usually inaccessible, as it's buried under the road."

Alan produced a pile of handouts. "Connor, isn't it? Would you hand these round please?" Alice noted the name. Connor's most obvious characteristic was his dark red hair; not only was he good looking, but he seemed friendly and good-natured into the bargain. Looks were not everything, although she was not impervious to physical allure; the folk she had met so far had all been friendly and she was amused by Dean, whose humour appealed to her. Switching her attention to the briefing papers she had only time to scan the first few lines before Professor Hughes began to speak.

"The original story is worth knowing from an archaeological point of view. The first surfaced road round the island wasn't built till 1873. When the workmen reached the west coast they had to remove a sand hill that was reported to be about twelve-foot-tall and sixty foot in circumference. That's about three point five metres by eighteen metres. Within that sand hill, a bronze age burial site was discovered; there were three burial cists empty apart from some black-looking sand and another black substance. Archaeology was a favourite pastime in Victorian times and the find was duly reported, recorded, mapped and photographed but the road took precedence and the site disappeared under the road once again until 1934 when there were further roadworks and the burial cists were once again exposed. This time, although they were again covered over, metal bars were placed in the road to mark their position. Your handout gives details and illustrations of the finds and extracts of how they were written up in journals.

"As you see from the time gap of sixty years between

the roadworks, uncovering the 1873 bronze age site rarely happens. Traffic on the island is light, mostly bicycles, and council budgets are hard strapped, so repairs are infrequent. But when it happens the bronze age site becomes news again. The last time the site was investigated was forty years ago in the nineteen seventies.

Our dig, however, is on a different site. The bronze age site has been thoroughly excavated and recorded. But, back in the seventies, Dr O'Flaherty and I were both part of a small additional archaeological dig in the east, opposite Largs and the mainland of Scotland. Our investigation focussed on a theory that there might be evidence of the Norse link with the island. King Haakon IV of Norway claimed all of the islands off the coast of Scotland and the Isle of Man.

We are fortunate to be able to reopen this site. We know that after the battle of Largs in 1263 the Norsemen collected their dead bodies and buried them. There is a record of one burial on the island of Bute, but there is no record of any of this having taken place on Cumbrae. We are particularly interested in trying to discover traces of Norse activity on Cumbrae.

"Ah, all our yesterdays." O'Flaherty intervened. "Both of us took part in that dig, as young aspiring academics, just starting out on our archaeological careers. We weren't cossetted in luxurious surroundings like this." He gestured expansively around the room. We had to bring our own tents. I well remember crawling into a minuscule bivouac tent. We hired ancient bikes with creaky gears and had lacerated ankles by the time we got to the site. Now we are bowed and balding, but our enthusiasm for the pursuit of the past is undiminished."

"A suitable note to end our first session. If you have any questions, unless they are urgent, I suggest you save them till tomorrow morning when we'll all meet at the dig site."

When they were left to their own devices, the students split into different groups, except for Henry Percy who went off to his own room, intending, he informed the others ponderously, to start working on his record book. Kathryn went off to play snooker with Connor and the twins, while Kenneth Matthews, who at sixty was the only mature student in the group, started to organise a darts tournament. The others drifted out for a final breath of air before turning in for the night.

Alice, Graziella, Dean and Paul strolled along in the direction of Millport, Paul having joined them at the invitation of Graziella who had seen him standing alone at the end of the pier opposite the Marine Biological Station. From their first meeting Dean had found Paul stand-offish and supercilious and this was exacerbated by what he considered the fluidity of his flirtatious overtures. In fairness though, as long as he didn't set his sights on Alice, Dean would be more tolerant. Unfortunately, Paul had already observed Dean's partiality for Alice and took an unholy pleasure in planning ways to annoy him.

Dean was quite proud of the adept way he had split Alice off from the others, by stopping at the imposing rock formation that jutted out from the hillside. Graziella and Paul already knew it, but as a new arrival Alice was intrigued and stopped to look more carefully, while the other two strolled on.

"It's a natural formation, but it looks like a gigantic lion from the right angle. It's called the Lion Rock, but that isn't a twentieth century name, like the Crocodile Rock. Its resemblance to a lion has been noted for centuries." Stop the lecture, he told himself. All of them had done their Google and Wikipedia research, he expected, including Alice, and this was no way to impress her. "It's getting dark. Let's stop here before the houses start," he said hopefully.

The beam of the lighthouse on Little Cumbrae flashed for three seconds and then went out for twenty. Another beam, darkness, another beam; the pulsing, signal unique to this spot, had been guiding navigators through the waters of the Firth of Clyde for more than a hundred years. Dean and Alice sat on the rocks at West Bay. Above them the steady light of the full moon cast its light over the sea. It was almost calm, only tiny waves breaking its surface and chopping the moonlight into silver ribbons.

❖ ❖ ❖

Next morning Alice woke early to a view across to the mainland of Scotland that, in one direction, was marred by the towers of Hunterston power station. It was better to look up-river to the north east towards Largs and the narrowing channel of the Firth of Clyde. Still she appreciated Mrs Macbeth's favouritism, as it was good to have access to a small common room just for the three girls. There was plenty of time for a breath of fresh air before their breakfast at half past seven.

On the pier opposite the hostel she met Connor and Paul. Connor greeted her affably. "I hear you're one of the few who know the history of the Viking period already. I hope they make allowances for total ignorance. Please rescue me if you see me heading for a cliff edge. All I know about Vikings is that they were buried at sea, sent off in splendid style in a burning boat."

"Not my period," Paul shrugged, before Alice had time to correct this stereotypical view of the Norsemen. "I'd rather excavate Egyptian or Roman ruins any time. I did try to find a similar dig somewhere on the Mediterranean. Better weather, better food, better vino in Italy" He grinned at Alice provocatively. "Bikinis," he said dreamily. "I can't see anyone bathing topless at Kames Bay in Millport, unless they're willing to risk a severe case of hypothermia."

Alice refused to be drawn. "I'll leave you to your puerile daydreams. If you want to risk the Doc's ire that's up to you. He seems genial, but I would bet that he has a nasty temper when roused. I suspect it wouldn't be a good idea to be in his bad books." Alice tucked her unruly curls into her woollen cap and turned back to the hostel for breakfast.

Indoors, the room was redolent of Ayrshire bacon and coffee. Kathryn had chosen the healthy option, orange juice and muesli with yoghurt, but a fascinated Graziella was being introduced to the delights of black pudding and potato scones.

"Ach aiblins it will be a dreich day the morn's morn," said

14

Paul, with a sideways glance at Matthias, who was chatting with Markus in German. Scots was not Paul's native tongue, but he was a natural mimic and had picked up a few stock phrases as party pieces at university in St Andrews.

Matthias regarded him with what the others later came to recognise as his signature impassive stare. Alice though was intrigued to see that Markus had tilted his chair back and was looking on with amusement, like someone anticipating entertainment.

"Could be," Matt shrugged. "But I thought the weather forecast was better than that."

Alice grinned appreciatively at this rejoinder. She had struggled a bit to understand Paul's remark, but she had got the gist from the Scots word 'dreich' that was so expressive that it denied satisfactory translation. "Did you study Scots as well as English?" she asked Matthias.

"One of our teachers at the Gymnasium was very keen on the poetry of Robert Burns. But our grannie was a Kennedy from Ayrshire, so we know how to pronounce Culzean and Auchtermuchty." Matthias smiled rarely, but when he did the likeness to Markus became even more startling.

"And," added Markus, "As grannie said, '*You dinna taigle wi a Kennedy*.' Although, if she heard him calling her grannie, he'd have had a skelp on the lug."

"I've understood only a fraction of that, but she sounds a formidable lady." Alice stood to take her breakfast tray back to the hatch and pick up one of the packed lunches that were stacked there.

"Aye." Matthias dropped the Scots word in deliberately, looking straight at Paul. "She was studying theology and German at Edinburgh University and did her year abroad in a small town near Heidelberg. She met and married the local minister and the result you see before you. I suppose we'd better be thinking of getting on our way." Obedient to the strictures of Mrs Macbeth, they trooped to the rack to return their trays before heading off to the dig.

The cyclists had a pleasant breeze from the south west behind them as they peddled along the coast road, the sight enhanced by the coloured sails of windsurf boards steered by learners from the water sports centre.

Two miles further on, Hughes and O'Flaherty were already on site, where Alan was showing the excavation preparations to his colleague Seamus O'Flaherty from Trinity College. Neither Alan nor Seamus stayed at the hostel. Mrs Macbeth was the resident warden, experienced at managing the students with a judicious blend of firmness and understanding, strengthened by excellent cooking and baking. It was better, they thought to preserve a degree of distance and privacy. Seamus had rented a flat on the main street of Millport. Alan had chosen to stay at the Cathedral of the Isles, where a former college had been turned into rather special bed and breakfast accommodation. Staying at the cathedral suited Alan. It meant a slightly longer journey in the morning, but it was nearer the museum, the library and *The Crocodile Rock*. He treasured the early morning when he could sit outside in the peaceful grounds and enjoy the tranquillity.

Clouds of pipe tobacco smoke rose upwards, as O'Flaherty examined the dig layout; tents, tarpaulins, a marquee and a couple of gaily striped gazebos.

"Space is limited," Alan observed. "We're lucky there's a flat area here. You'll remember from the last dig that often there's very little ground between the hills and the coastline and what there is can be marshy. You could say the spot was well chosen for a burial, if any of the Norsemen were in fact buried on Cumbrae." He looked calculatingly at Seamus. It was many years since they had met as students on a similar archaeological dig, but their paths had rarely crossed since then. Rising to a professorship in Scotland had occupied much of his time and Hughes had only occasionally come across O'Flaherty's name in the interim. "Once the students arrive, could you tuck your pipe away? Technically this is a place of work so smoking is out. The lot we have don't seem particularly bolshie, but best not court objections."

"Suppose I argue it's a midge deterrent?" Seamus suggested, before good-naturedly pocketing the briar pipe.

"I think there's a strong enough aroma of tobacco to have the whole midge population of Cumbrae dashing for the Largs ferry." Alan countered. "Do you often set your pocket alight with that thing?"

"It has been known. I see the topsoil has been removed from areas we didn't excavate on our dig in the dim and distant past. I thought that was best, as we'll be starting afresh at those spots. Right let's have a look at your preparations and set things up for the morning briefing." It wasn't long before the sound of bicycles blended with the cry of sea birds and lapping waves. Soon after, the first session of the day got off to a brisk start.

"Forget the horned helmets." Hughes was aware that most of the group had not studied the period. "Haakon's seal presents him as a medieval knight on a prancing high spirited horse. He is wearing a barrel helm, the type of head protection worn by crusaders of the time. There may have been an element of flattery in the design, but this gift, from Henry III of England was a clear message that Haakon was considered a Christian knight, part of the chivalric hierarchy."

Alice looked closely at the two lecturers. The obvious physical dissimilarity was marked. O'Flaherty was bearded beneath high coloured cheeks, with an infectious grin. Hughes was thinner, paler and more serious; on his left hand he wore a broad gold wedding ring. O'Flaherty had none, but that didn't mean he was unmarried, Alice thought; some men, particularly of the older generation, chose not to wear a ring. Not that it mattered; it was just one point of difference between the men. More important was the contrast in manner. O'Flaherty radiated an air of jocular bonhomie. Hughes did smile, but fleetingly, his normal expression one of placid gravity.

His description of the background to the events of 1263 was delivered, however, with full dramatic effect.

"The sea out there would have been full of Viking longships." Hughes gestured to the canvas flap of the tent door that had been looped up to allow a view to the east, across the narrow strip of water separating Greater Cumbrae from the mainland of Scotland and the town of Largs. "Haakon's foreign policy was based on a show of force that terrified his opponents into submission. When you have time to walk round the island a bit to the west you'll see the island of Bute, just opposite. It had already felt the force of a Norse attack. The castle had been taken and the garrison slaughtered."

All of the students had visited battle sites. They had felt the special force that this lent to their understanding of the human stories that had played out on the ground beneath their feet. As Hughes spoke, he fired their imagination and the waters of the Clyde became full of intimidating longships, with their coloured sails and terrifying carved prows.

"It was the most formidable force that had ever left Norway," Alan continued. "The contemporary sagas make that quite clear. These were no illiterate savages. Haakon had been educated at Bergen Cathedral school and his court would have compared favourably with any in Europe. But he considered all the Western Isles as his territory and that included the two Cumbraes, Bute and Arran. When he heard that King Alexander III of Scotland was trying to claim them he set out to consolidate his influence over all the islands."

"Forget also any pictures of a few longships out on a raid." O'Flaherty took up the tale. "Imagine hundreds of ships of different sizes. Haakon's flagship was a symbol of his power. It was built of oak, with twenty-seven banks of oars. The gilded dragons and sea serpents were there to evoke awe and terror." He paused to nod at Connor, who had raised his hand.

"I'm still learning about this period, so sorry if this is a dumb question, but how do we know all this?"

"Good question. We'll look at sources and their reliability later. We know the names of his companions and his crew. Every oar was rowed by four men. We even know where they were berthed. On the quarter deck Thorlife, the abbot of Holm, with four priests, Andrew Hawardson, Erik Dugalson, Wilfrid Lang-bard, Fri Scolbein - the muster list goes on and on. Haakon had personally selected those who would be aboard his flagship."

"The women relegated to a passive role, waving handker-chiefs as the fleet departed," muttered Alice in an undertone. She knew that the latest research challenged the idea that the Vikings had left their women behind, but she had to admit that it was most likely that they brought their families only once they had decided to settle elsewhere. It was highly unlikely that there was a woman on board Haakon's fleet, but, in the warmth of the tent, the tangy odour of the nearby sea, the flap of the canvas above she slipped into a daydream of the might have been.

BERGEN 1263

Ragnhild and Harald

Bergen was a bustling port that had eased into its position as capital of Norway during Haakon's rule. When he secured the throne, he had strengthened the fortress and made it the centre of his administration. Trondheim, the seat of his challengers to the throne, the Nideros, had lost its status and Bergen had expanded as traders plied between Norway and the rest of Europe.

Ragnhild Haakonsdottir loved to wander by herself around the harbour, watching grain being unloaded, observing how the crews moored or cast off. She stroked the furs that lay in piles waiting to be loaded and imagined them being used to trim cloaks in some foreign city. She smiled as she saw the heads of the harbour seals bob up and down, in anticipation of snapping titbits, as the women gutting the cod threw the offal into the water before beginning the salting. Some of the women, recognising her from her regular visits wished her a cheerful, 'heil ok sæl' as she strolled on.

She walked by herself, but not alone. She knew that, behind her, karls would be following as discreetly as two hefty guards could do. The serfs were watchful, but there was no need for great vigilance. Haakon's reputation protected her from annoyance. Everyone knew who she was. Ragnhild dressed simply: her woollen gown was plain with no fine trimming; her hair was twisted into loose braids. But the gown was of the finest wool; the sleeves were wider than would be practical for any girl whose duties included everyday chores; she bore herself with a confidence that inspired deference. Even a stranger would quickly realise she was a person of some importance.

A karvi rounded the harbour and glided smoothly towards

the moorings some distance from the trading ships. Ragnhild's eyes sparkled and she started to run along the wooden walkway towards the shallower water. She watched appreciatively, as the steersman brought his craft alongside expertly.

Ragnhild's family was complicated. Although not particularly promiscuous, her father had sired a brood of children, in and out of wedlock. Ragnhild raised her head proudly. She herself was not the child of Haakon and his wife Margarete.

In truth she was one of the latter breed. Haakon and his queen Margarete had three children, two sons and a daughter but Ragnhild had been brought into the family so young that all three children regarded her as their little sister. She knew several other half brothers and sisters. There were undoubtedly quite a few more scattered around the kingdom, but most of Haakon's other offspring stayed with their mothers.

Her own mother had died as she was born and it had been her good fortune that Haakon had bonded with the tiny orphaned infant. He had brought her to Margarete and she, with her usual placid acceptance, had included her in the family and treated her like her other children. Ragnhild had always regarded her as her mother. The youngest child in the nursery, Ragnhild had been doted on by eight-year-old Magnus and fourteen-year-old Haakon, who had already been declared a junior king. Twelve-year-old Christina already considered herself grown-up and preferred the company of her mother and the other ladies. But the boys had been fascinated by the little creature and, as she grew up, they encouraged her to take part in their wild romps. Now Christina was married and Magnus was Haakon's heir and junior king."

Her favourite had been Haakon, the eldest. Now six years dead, he remained vivid in her memory. 'The best horseman in Norway.' The bards were paid to flatter and exaggerate, but with Haakon the truth had been enough. Handsome and brim-full of energy and charm, he would only have been thirty now. As she grew up, he had been a source of joy in her life. He and his wife Rikitsa had given her a first nephew, young Sverre. Now Sverre was also dead and Rikitsa back in her native Sweden.

"Hey," a voice protested. "Why the long face? Don't know that it is the duty of landlubbers to greet returning heroes with smiles and wreaths of welcome?" Harald Haakonsfostri jumped lithely ashore and turned to catch a bundle tossed to him by one of the crew. Leaving the others to secure the craft, he swung into step beside Ragnhild, shortening his long stride to match hers. "So, sister, have you been haunting the shore, watching avidly for a sight of my sail?"

Yes, it was complicated. Harald was not her brother. In fact, he was not a blood relation at all, but was her foster brother, son of a Jarl who had supported Haakon in the civil war. When Jarl Erik had died, fighting at Haakon's side, the King had generously taken the boy and raised him at his court. Now twenty, he occupied the place in Ragnhild's life once held by her half-brother, now dead. They had an easy friendship, bolstered by his readiness to help her evade her stepmother's attempts to tame her.

As they neared the main landing jetties, the smell of fish became stronger. The gulls wheeled overhead crying raucously, anticipating the bounty of fish heads to come.

"Well you've had your chance. Still, I like silence in a woman." Harald teased. "Now you'll have to listen to my travels. You should have seen the size of the basking shark that got away."

Ragnhild smiled at him derisively and prepared to be amused. He always told a good tale.

Growing up at the court of her father, King Haakon IV of Norway, Ragnhild knew herself to be both pampered and imprisoned. She knew she was her father's favourite daughter. One upward glance through her long eyelashes, one pretty smile and she could achieve her ends. This man who aroused terror at home and abroad would smile fondly and agree to her whim of the moment.

Her elder sister, Christina, had been her mother's faithful companion before she left for Spain. Christina had her mother's personality and shared her interests. King Henry III of England was well advised when he sent Queen Margarete two gifts of sumptuous red fabric. Together Christina and her mother planned how these could be made into stylish clothes, gowns and mantles fitting for the court of a powerful ruler, who in his long reign had become a major player on the European stage. Ragnhild abhorred her needle and resented time spent cutting up fabric, only to sew it together into a different shape. She wanted to ride, to run and above all to sail.

Although Haakon held traditional views on the place of women, he was proud of his intrepid young daughter, whose eyes gleamed in delight as their small craft crested the waves. He prided himself on his seamanship. A ruler who stood at the prow of the flagship of the most powerful fleet in the world must be able to command the respect of a seafaring nation. King since the age of thirteen, Haakon could sail and steer single-handed, take his place at a bank of oars and fry fish on the shore in genial companionship with his crew. He was also a ruthless killer, when the occasion demanded it.

But that was a side of her father's character that Ragnhild did not see. She never displeased him, so she remained his sweetest flower, indulged and encouraged in a way that troubled her mother. Margarete was not impressed that her younger daughter could gut and fillet a fish, light a fire, climb a tree to search the horizon for homecoming longships. There were servants to do that; it was unbecoming in a princess. When Ragnhild argued pertly that there were plenty of seamstresses to do the sewing, Margarete sighed but said nothing. She no longer tried to bring her wayward daughter into line, either by punishment or by persuasion. The girl was impossible and Margarete liked a quiet life.

For much of her youth Ragnhild did not worry about marriage. She knew it would be something over which she had little control. Princesses were currency in the marriage market, an asset to be used to expand the realm, or increase its security. But her father didn't seem anxious to dispose of his daughters in marriage. Her sister Christina had been twenty-four when she was married to Philipe of Castile. At present Haakon was content to have his lively younger daughter at his side, laughing at his wit, making him laugh in turn and listening avidly to his tales of adventurous voyages. Ragnhild wondered if the circumstances of his own marriage explained this. Queen Margarete had been scarcely nine when she was married to the fourteen-year-old Haakon almost forty years ago, although the actual ceremony took place six years later. How happy their union had been, Ragnhild did not know. Outwardly they put on a good show of unity when about their royal duties. What Margarete had felt when her father was killed by Haakon was also unknown. Earl Skule Bardsson had been the regent, ruling Norway during Haakon's minority, and her marriage was designed to strengthen their bond, but when the earl declared himself king, he was burnt to death when Haakon's men set fire to the monastery where he was seeking sanctuary. Margarete never spoke about her family, accepted Haakon's infidelities and bore Haakon four children.

Harald and Ragnhild parted at St Mary's church: She smiled at him and slipped quietly into the building; Harald gave a friendly nod to the two housekarls, tacitly acknowledging their duty to protect the princess. As Ragnhild made her way to the Lady Chapel to offer a prayer, the housekarls stood rather uncomfortably near the back wall. One reached to the talisman that hung round his neck on a leather thong. Christianity had been well established in the Northern kingdoms for centuries. Silversmiths did a steady trade in pendants with a cruciform design; but the canny craftsmen still had moulds with images of Thor's hammer. King Haakon was tolerant of the men who wore them tucked discreetly under their tunic. It was a sign of superstition, a legacy from a former age kept alive by old sagas and songs, rather than an alternative religion. All men cried to God in a storm and the old gods had buckled under the onslaught of the Christian creed.

CUMBRAE 2005

W ith some reluctance, Alice turned her attention to the present, as Professor Hughes described the schedule for that day. "First we will start dry sieving the cuttings that have been opened for us by a local farmer with his JCB. We'll work a rotation, with five excavating on the site and two in the tent, ready to record finds and observations. You'll find exemplars of how that is done inside the tent. The other three of you will work in the Museum of the Cumbraes in the Garrison, the imposing building in the centre of Millport. Today I'll be on site, while Dr O'Flaherty will be at the museum, where you'll find some material already set out for you by the archivist. Bad weather is central to the story of Haakon's fleet at the battle of Largs, and, while we have no visual record of that actual event in the illustrated manuscripts of the time, you'll find some evidence of what stormy weather can do to this normally sheltered town and harbour. Look out for the pictures from 1912, when there was a devastating storm that caused great damage. This will give you some idea of the kind of conditions that Norse fleet had to withstand."

"Glad we're starting with the clean option." Paul lined up his bicycle beside Kathryn, who had already wheeled her vehicle briskly into the road. Together they set off along the coastal road, the Firth of Clyde on their left and bracken-covered hills on their right. Behind them, Kenneth Matthews pedalled sedately as befitted the oldest member of the group.

Already retired, he was fulfilling a lifetime ambition by enrolling on a part-time university course. He had two grandchildren who were the same age as his fellow students and he observed their youthful antics with indulgence.

◆ ◆ ◆

At the dig the mood was jovial.

"For the first hour everyone will be excavating, working in pairs. I'll demonstrate the procedure as we go. Later, as the soil and debris build up, we'll make a start on the testing and recording side of things. Connor, you and I will work together to show the others the basic techniques. Then I'll leave you with..." he paused and glanced round, "with Matthias, while I get the rest started off."

To his delight Dean found himself working with Alice. Hughes next paired himself with Henry, while Markus and Graziella made up the fourth team. These teams were fluid, however, as Hughes joined each in turn, sending one person off to join the last person he had worked with.

"It's like a progressive barn dance," Dean muttered when he found himself working with Connor. He would, of course, have preferred a whole morning getting to know Alice.

"Sure it's just to mix us up and let us get to know one another. What's the music scene like in Glasgow?"

The tactic worked. When Hughes arrived to oust Connor, they had moved on from music and were deep in conversation about rugby and the performances of the Scottish and Irish teams in the Six Nations Championship.

They had made good progress, Dean thought, as Hughes squatted beside him to discuss how to identify different soil types and contents. This was the last team change of the morning and a quick stroll with Alice at lunchtime was his latest aim. He had spotted a large heron on his way to the dig. He wondered if she was more interested in birds than biscuits.

Lunchtime found Paul and Kathryn perched on a seat near

both *The Crocodile Rock* pub and the real Crocodile Rock, a rock painted to look like a crocodile which was a favourite choice for family photographs. In its million-year existence perhaps some ancient inhabitants of the island had noticed its shape at high tide and linked it to a sea monster. Its most recent history was that it had acquired its painted teeth and mouth early in the twentieth century, when a regular to the nearby pub had pointed it out to his cronies on emerging at closing time, but had failed to persuade them of the similarity. Needled by the derision of the others he had returned with paint brushes and pots and the islanders rose the next morning to an eye catching amphibian that stretched its open mouth towards the shore. Since then it had become an icon, visitors from all over the world coming to have their photograph taken on it.

Paul produced a small camera from his backpack. "It's irresistible, isn't it? Would you like a souvenir photograph?" A few moments later Kathryn was perched on the crocodile's back, ready to be recorded for posterity like thousands before her.

"Would you like me to take a photo of both of you?" a man on the stone jetty offered. His children had been clambering over the rock when Kathryn and Paul arrived and were now exploring rock pools nearby.

Paul looked at Kathryn, who nodded. "I'll finish the film and try to get it developed, so that you can have it before we go home. Or if you give me your address I can send them on." He felt he was making progress. Kathryn was not exactly encouraging, but she was far less stand-offish than she had been earlier.

In the pub opposite, Kenneth Matthews had eschewed his packed lunch in favour of pub grub. Behind the bar the licensee Martin McCrone was emptying the coffee grounds from his latest acquisition. He remembered the days when no self-respecting Scottish pub would have served coffee, but you needed to move with the times. The spit and sawdust days of the male-only Scottish pub were over. Martin had to admit that the income from hot drinks and food made the investment in a state of the art coffee machine worthwhile. Now he was listening sceptically to yet another innovative idea his son was suggesting.

"*Irish* music?" Martin looked at his son dubiously. "You think that would draw folk in? It's not exactly authentic Cumbrae culture."

"Come off it, dad. I don't remember Miss Farquharson telling us about cowboys riding around the island when we were doing local history at primary school. But the Country and Western event is great for business. The whole place is packed." Fraser knew his father would always listen to an idea that could attract more customers. "I've been talking to one of these students. He plays the banjo and I thought he might agree to play at the mid-week Talent Night. Turns out there's quite a bit of amateur talent amongst them. If they could get up a group, we could probably get a live music event just for the cost of a few pints of Guinness."

"A few pints." Martyn hadn't dropped the tone of scepticism but Fraser knew he had captured his father's attention. Anything that had a promise of profit was certain to get a hearing. "A keg more like, if I know anything about students. And there'll be no Irish whiskey. Nothing spelled with a superfluous *e* will ever be served in this establishment. I told that Irish teacher of theirs, Scotch whisky or nothing. We must have some standards."

Fraser grinned. He had made the suggestion. He would let it alone and wait to see how long it was before his father mentioned it again, probably having convinced himself it was his own idea.

That evening, in their cosy sitting room, Graziella, Alice and Kathryn snatched a moment to chat about their first day on the project before the evening meal. When they updated Kathryn, both Alice and Graziella were enthusiastic about their day at the dig site.

"We started right into it. I was sorry I missed the visit yesterday, but it didn't really matter. The prof certainly got us down to work quickly. Everything seems well organised. I like how we are doing stints on excavation and stints on the other tasks like recording."

Graziella smiled, "Me, I don't mind the digging. My family are farmers. My grandmother gave us hoes and shovels from an early age. *Nonna* was determined we would learn how to grow things. Although I liked it better when we went out to hunt for wild strawberries."

"My grandparents were determined their children wouldn't wield shovels," Kathryn observed. "They wanted their family to do well at school and get an education. Coal mining was dangerous and dirty. Today, when we were sent into Millport, Paul said we had been given the clean option."

"I take it that suited him." Alice was not yet sure how she felt about Paul.

"I suppose so. We'll see how he copes with digging tomorrow. At least the weather is set to be good all week. I can't imagine excavating would be much fun in mud and rain."

"We'll be putting up tarpaulin shelters tomorrow, the professor said. But, believe it or not, it's to give us shade, as it's due to be pretty hot. Best not forget the sun cream," Alice advised.

"They seem to be settling in quite well," Alan Hughes said, as he and his colleague surveyed the assembled group, chatting easily as they took their seats.

The last session of the day was brief, the idea being that it would finish early enough to allow everyone to adjourn to *The Crocodile Rock* if they wished. The plan was that the students' schedule would always include a short seminar on the historical background to the period, to highlight selected issues. Hughes and O'Flaherty were programmed to lead on alternate days and this first evening it was O'Flaherty's turn.

"*Hier stehe Ich. Ich kann nicht anders. Gott helfe mir.*" O'Flaherty declaimed. "That more or less sums up the attitude of Alexander III to the Isles of Cumbrae. If you can't immediately translate Martin Luther's words, no doubt someone from the group can enlighten you."

Alan smiled despite himself. The man was good. His dramatic interludes grasped his student audience. And kept them entertained. O'Flaherty looked expectantly towards the twins, neither of whom reacted.

"*Here I stand. I cannot do otherwise. May God help me.*" Dean hated himself for not resisting the impulse, for always needing to prove his superiority to Paul. "But it's probably a legend. There's no evidence he ever said that." O'Flaherty cast a look of dislike at Dean. Students who did not succumb to his charm were not popular with him.

"Like Luther, King Alexander had a sticking point. Haakon claimed all the Scottish islands. Alexander was more or less reconciled to the fact that he could not yet win the struggle for the larger, more northerly islands, but he refused to give up the Cumbraes, Arran and Bute. And he was prepared to fight."

Confident of the effectiveness of his cliff-hanger ending, O'Flaherty bowed briefly, lifted an imaginary beer glass to his lips, and left the room.

There was time to cycle into Millport, an option followed by Connor, Graziella and Kenneth, but some opted to stay put and just relax, although Henry Percy immediately disappeared to his room. The others congregated in the common-room. It was functional rather than attractive. Sofas and armchairs were grouped in two large squares around coffee tables. One wall held a flat screen television; another had French windows looking out on a neatly tended garden. Tables and chairs were pushed against the other two walls, except for a space where a hatch led to the kitchen. An automatic urn, a small fridge and a cupboard for mugs and glasses stood nearby.

Why did you come too? Paul asked Markus, having learned that, although both twins were at Heidelberg university, only Matthias was studying archaeology, as part of a classics degree. Markus was a second year medical student. "Is it a twin thing?" he continued. "Joined at the hip?"

Two impassive gazes confronted him, the dark brown eyes and eyebrows an unusual combination with fair hair.

"No," said Matthias, with mock patience. "That is Siamese twins. We are identical twins, but perhaps you don't know the difference?"

"Actually I have always wondered about twins." Alice's intervention eased the palpable tension between Paul and the twins. "We are quite a large family, so I have lots of brothers and sisters, but there are no twins in the family. It must be special to be a twin. What's it like to have someone who looks the same as you do? Do you like the same things? Have you ever swapped places?"

"We like some of the same things," Matthias shrugged.

"Of course we have," Markus answered. The responses came simultaneously,

"What's the point of looking alike if you can't have some fun?" Markus went on.

Alice examined their expressions closely. "Actually I think you *are* different. Matt looks more," she paused. "More serious. You, I think, are more reckless."

"That's perceptive." Matthias took up the conversation. "I think you might be right. We both like sport, but Markus likes rock climbing. I see absolutely no point in clambering up some perilous overhang, if there is a perfectly easy alternative path."

"So do you like ping-pong?" Paul seemed totally unable to prevent himself goading people, but Matthias refused to respond to the taunt.

"Gymnastics is my sport, but we do have a top-class table tennis club at home. When you see them practise it's impressive, the pace, the athleticism, the quick-thinking." His brother was less conciliatory.

"Everybody's view of sport is different. Perhaps you prefer hopscotch - or dominoes?"

Matthias shook his head despairingly at his twin's intervention. "*Kind, du bist nicht zu retten.*" Used to being told he was beyond rescuing, Markus grinned unrepentantly and watched as his twin rose to his feet.

Markus returned his coffee cup to the trolley. "I'm going for a run. I'll see you all later. *Tschüß.*"

❖ ❖ ❖

Dawn had a particular charm on Cumbrae. As Alan sat outside the cloisters of the Cathedral of the Isles, the wind rose slightly and the distinctive cry of the nuthatch was now accompanied by the rustle of leaves on the branches of the sycamores. *Whee whee whee whee whee.* Sometimes five calls, sometimes three. Alan counted them idly and wondered if there was some secret code determining the bird's choice of rhythm. In a field nearby, a cow lowed steadily.

The tall elegant spire of the Cathedral rose confidently in the sky. Each side of the tower was pierced by three pointed gothic windows and indeed the Cathedral, completed in 1851, had been deliberately built in the style of the 13th century; so, Alan mused, it would not have been so different to the edifices that both Alexander and Haakon would have known. The cockerel and the arrow on the weathervane showed that the last time it had turned a westerly wind had been blowing.

The bell of the cathedral chimed the quarter hour. Alan rose to go, fully persuaded that the initial rough ride to get to the main road was a price worth paying for the serenity of the surroundings.

BERGEN 1263

Her devotions over, Ragnhild resigned herself to her mother's recriminations. They met in the herb garden where Margarete grew mint, rosemary and basil. The sweet-smelling and health-giving plants flourished in the shelter of the thick walls of the fortress, the clear blue of the flowering basil bright against the grey walls. Ragnhild crushed a sprig of rosemary in her hand. "I was at the church, mother," she said evasively, her equivocation a sin to be included in her next confession.

"No doubt." Margarete knew her daughter. "Is that why you smell like a fishwife?"

Ragnhild bit back a pert reply. Our blessed Lord went fishing, she thought. And He cooked fish for his disciples on the seashore. He would be quite at home at the harbour, she reflected. But she said nothing. Later, in her chamber, she added some of her mother's rose-water to the washbasin her maid had brought.

Despite herself, she grinned; her mother's fishwife taunt had taken effect. It was time to resume the role of a young lady, modest, demure and fragrant.

From a window overlooking the herb garden Haakon smiled at his daughter's slim figure as she gathered a posy of sweet scented flowers and herbs, then frowned as he turned back into his chamber.

"Alexander, King of Scots," Haakon growled. "He's like a burr under my tunic. He cannot inflict a deep wound, but his scratches draw blood. His raids on the Northern Isles are intolerable. The Hebrides are mine. It is well time I stirred myself and dealt with him."

Magister William, his chaplain, regarded him keenly. "Alex-

ander would say, as King of Scots, he is only bringing his unruly subjects to heel."

"A hopeless task. These island chiefs are ungovernable. Alexander has no means of reaching them, far less subduing them. They have their galleys, their feuds, their alliances. Alaxandair mac Alaxandair" Haakon spoke the king's Gaelic name proudly. He liked to display his linguistic skills and found them helpful when aiming to impress. "No, he cannot rule them from the Scottish mainland. Even I cannot rule them, although I have far more sea power. But I can collect their tribute, settle their disputes, wring from them a grudging acknowledgement of my suzerainty over them."

He rose and made his way to the narrow window, overlooking the busy harbour. "Of course I know that the minute my ships are over the horizon these petty rulers will do as they please. But at least those longships will be laden with tribute that I have extracted from them. No, I cannot be seen to ignore Alexander's incursions into my territories. It is decided."

He turned back to look steadily at William, his confessor and his friend. "We sail after midsummer. No doubt Alexander has word of our preparations. Even although I prevented Alexander's spy, the Scotsman Missel, from leaving Norway, traders' gossip will have filtered through to him. I shall send word to Magnus Olafson of the Isle of Man, to Iceland, Orkney and Shetland, and to Ewan MacDougall of Lorn and his like. I shall make it clear that I expect the support of the northern and southern isles. Thank you for your advice, my friend."

William smiled at the mild irony and rose to follow Haakon to the scriptorium where letters to his allies would be prepared and copied.

CUMBRAE 2005

Henry Percy looked up nervously like a deer startled by the arrival of a hiker. Connor's suggestion had caught him as he was about to scuttle away.

"Fancy a game of snooker tonight?"

"Uh, no thanks, I thought I'd write up today's notes then." He glanced at the door as if searching for an escape route, before leaving with a placatory grin.

"He doesn't want to want to join in anything. "Graziella exclaimed in exasperation. "We've all tried, well most of us." She shot an accusatory look at Paul, who shrugged coolly.

From the outset, Ken Matthews and Henry Percy had stood apart from the others in different ways. Ken had children older than any of them and an adventurous life and a long career behind him. But he was comfortable in the company of young people and popular with them. Henry Percy fitted in less well. Any friendly inquiry about his interests seemed to startle him into incoherence and his steady refusal of all invitations discouraged their attempts to include him.

The second day saw Alice, Matthias and Henry sent off to meet Professor Hughes at the Museum in Millport while the others worked at the site. Research seemed to suit Henry and he opted to study through the lunch hour rather than join Alice and Matthias for a stroll along towards the harbour. They talked easily as they went.

"I find this place so calm, Matthias said. "Yet those photographs of storms show the force of the sea, when it's aroused. The weather is to be good for the whole dig. Not *dreich* at all," he chuckled.

"Dean and Markus should just ignore Paul," Alice observed. "It just encourages him, if he succeeds in annoying people."

At the site, it was O'Flaherty's turn to lead the team.

"Dig, dig, dig, dig, dig, dig, dig," O'Flaherty sang by way of introduction. "You are on a carefully constructed rota, so that each one of you gets a turn at basic excavation techniques, sieving, giving the exact coordinates of a find, photographing and describing the find, making sketch map records and so on, with everything recorded in your log books, which will be submitted with your final reports."

"So no pressure then," muttered Connor in an undertone.

They had been well warned to expect lots of painstaking work, examining soil with little chance of dramatic finds. But, against all the odds, Tuesday brought an exciting discovery. Alice was working with Connor. At the outer edge of the cutting, a small artefact jutted from the earth that she was meticulously brushing. It was clearly not a pebble and what shape could be distinguished showed a rounded disc, with a cylindrical stem.

All of the standard procedures were set in action. The exact location was logged and the position tagged. Photographs were taken at each stage of the extraction and it was transported carefully to the marquee for further examination.

"What can it possibly be?" asked Kathryn as they grouped round the object. "It's obviously an artefact, but what could it be *for*? I've never seen anything that shape."

"I'm no expert in this period." Connor Crozier seemed diffident about expressing an opinion, but obviously felt he had something to add. "I play the banjo and to me it looks awfully like a tuning peg for winding the wire round to tune an instrument." He pointed to a small hole that was bored through the stem.

"So you think it's modern?"

"Not necessarily. I don't suppose the shape has altered much over centuries, just perhaps the materials. That could be made of bronze and I suppose carbon dating could give us more information."

O'Flaherty was impressed. "That's an inspired guess and you are right that there are some basic tools that have changed little over millennia. I seem to remember a find of a broken harp peg in Ireland. We can look it up and see if there's any similarity. If it is a broken peg, though, there is no guarantee the original instrument is nearby. Many findings are of things discarded because they are no longer useful, catgut strings would have rotted and any wooden structure would have disintegrated.

The potential tuning peg remained their only solid find that day, however. It was frustrating too that the find had been at the furthest extent of the cutting. It would have been interesting to extend the cutting, but O'Flaherty was adamant that was not an option open to the students. He had a site plan of where they were to excavate and no additional areas were to be examined. They had to be content with knowing that they had notched up the first significant discovery of the dig.

BERGEN 1263

Harald carefully removed the gittern from his sea chest and laid it on the floor beside his bed, before flinging himself full length onto the mattress. Some words of a new song had come to him during the morning's sail, some fragments of a possible tune. He wanted to work at them while he could still remember and while he had the place to himself. Painstakingly he began to tune the instrument.

Living arrangements in the Bergenhus fortress followed fairly fixed rules. The uppermost floor housed the royal family. Haakon and his wife had apartments at the south side, reached by their own staircase, a haven of privacy for those who had to pass most of their lives in public. Bedrooms were not over-large. Although Haakon did a certain amount of business in his private quarters, this was limited to meetings with his closest friends and advisers, a small trusted group.

The hall on the ground floor was in constant use. Formerly the main hall, it was still a busy place with housekarls and serving-maids crossing back and forth constantly, strewing fresh rushes or sweeping away debris. A large, much more prestigious structure, Haakonshall, replaced it. Gothic in design, with its own cellar and ample space to receive embassies and hold large gatherings, the new hall was intended to impress, to show visiting noblemen and dignitaries that Norway could compete in culture and prestige with any southern land.

As Haakon's foster son, and one of his elite band of young noblemen, Harald merited a space on an upper floor. He shared a chamber on the north side with three others. It was simply furnished: a trestle table with some bowls and drinking horns; beds with woollen palliasses, filled with straw. Six chests, which were used as benches on long voyages, provided seating and some personal storage.

The group had been together since their schooldays, when they had all attended the Bergen Cathedral School. From childhood they had played like wolf cubs, buffeting one another softly, racing, wrestling, but with no animosity and few disagreements. There was no natural leader in the group: Bjorgvin excelled on skis, Harald on horseback; Torvig liked to argue; Erik liked a quiet life.

Harald had no interest in becoming either a priest or a clerk, but the Cathedral School no longer existed only to train boys for the priesthood. Nobles and aspiring freemen saw the benefit of subjecting their sons to a basic education in Latin and literacy. Haakon himself had been to the same school and actively encouraged his jarls to educate their sons.

Harald was still in the throes of composition when the chamber door was thrown open. As it banged back loudly against the stone wall he laid the gittern aside, resigned to the knowledge that his time of creativity was over.

"So here you are, skulking on your own. It's not healthy. Haven't you read in 'The King's Mirror' that idleness is a sin, to be avoided by the young man of ambition?"

"No I haven't, because it isn't in it. But I do remember it says something about treating doors with respect and trying not to burst their hinges just to enter a room. While you have been bumbling around the town, dallying with any damsel too slow to outrun you, I have been raiding the bounty of the sea, catching plump fish for the table."

"Yes, Eda the fishwife told me you had bought a string of sardines." Bjorgvin eyed the gittern. "A new tune? Any good?" Although they cultivated an air of nonchalance, Bjorgvin and the others took music seriously, proud of their friend's talent. The gittern was Harald's pride and joy, the latest musical instrument in all Europe and favoured by troubadours and amateurs alike.

"I think so." Harald liked to use Bjorgvin as a sounding board. He could rely on his honesty and valued his suggestions.

"It's still only a rough idea, but I think at least a fragment of it is worthwhile." His fingers flew adroitly over the strings in demonstration of the section he was most pleased with.

By evening it was a full band of four that emerged from the room, ready to perform their duties as attentive young squires at Haakon's table. One by one the others had trailed in to have a perfunctory wash, drag a bone comb through their fashionable curls and dress appropriately for their evening roles.

Now that they had left the Cathedral school, Magister William supervised their training. Some said the Englishman had written 'The King's Mirror' - a book of advice for a young man making his way in the world, choosing a career and deciding on the principles that would guide him through life. Although the author of the book had chosen to be anonymous, it could only have been written by someone well-travelled, well-versed in the latest scientific knowledge of the world, well-acquainted with the Holy Scriptures and with the Norse sagas. In the story, a king of a Northern kingdom draws on his knowledge and experience to answer questions from his son, seasoning his serious advice with stories of adventures and wonders, to keep his audience interested. He describes far-off lands that were nonetheless not so far away that they were beyond the reach of the intrepid Norse sailors. Whilst Magister William was learned enough to provide much of the text, the sections on seafaring showed a knowledge that would have come more easily from Haakon.

Harald had found that much of the advice on how to conduct yourself in the presence of a king was identical with the etiquette that Haakon expected of him and his companions. Their training encompassed rules for mind and body and most of it made sense to him, although there were some odd prohibitions; a warning against harlots was understandable but Harald and the others found it amusing that it was in a list that also advised against playing chess. Young men were expected to choose leisure activities that would help them become warriors, sailors and useful loyal subjects of the king.

CUMBRAE 2005

In the marquee the tuning peg was taken to the tent, where Kathryn, Matthias and Dean set to work to record it, laying it on coloured cloth to photograph, with small measurement markers to show its size. The data was entered into their laptop computer and then O'Flaherty sent the three back to the hostel research room to print out the photographs and to make copies of the records for each of the group. The others continued their dry sieving, hopeful, but ultimately unsuccessful.

"I've done some climbing in the Dolomites, but not rock climbing, more hill-walking really," Graziella said casually to Markus, as they collected photocopies and organised them into ten bundles on the research room table. "Do you think the cliffs would be any good for a beginner?"

Markus shrugged, "I don't think so. I looked it up before I came and although on the mainland near Largs there are some possibilities, there is nothing on Cumbrae. The walk to the top of the island is just a gentle slope, apparently. Matt has already done a circular run there. It looks as if the best sport is in or on the water, although it's a bit colder here than Italy. If you like, though, there's maybe a bit of bouldering on the rock behind the hostel. We can have a look at the cliffs on the west side of the island, as well, when we get a bit of time off."

Since they were already back at the hostel there was time to have a stroll outside and have a look at the rock Markus had mentioned, before the others returned for the next briefing. As they were examining the rock surface, some of the others arrived back. Matthias parked his bicycle in the rack, with a shake of his head at his twin, but O'Flaherty wandered over to the couple, inwardly envying them their youth and agility.

"Not good territory for climbing," he observed, shaking his head, thinking back gloomily to a time when he too had been able to climb uphill effortlessly, a time before a sedentary lifestyle and a love of the good life made itself evident on his body.

◆ ◆ ◆

Once again the evening session was short and everyone decided to celebrate their find with a drink in Millport. Graziella was enthusiastic about the town. She was determined to notch up as many 'typically Scottish' experiences as she could on this visit, but she had also been delighted to find there was a strong Italian influence on the island. For generations there had been Italian families running popular businesses, ice cream cafes, fish and chip shops. She had yet to try the fish and chips, but already was mooting the idea of a special carry-out one evening.

"Do you think Mrs Macbeth would be insulted, if we brought in our own food?" She was a kindly soul and genuinely cared about other people's feelings.

"I'm sure she won't mind, as long as we give her plenty of notice. It'll give her some extra time off."

When the others arrived at *The Crocodile Rock* that evening Matt was already seated in a corner nook with half a pint of lager. It had been an easy run, flat all the way. On his left the Firth of Clyde ran towards the Irish Sea. Landward, steep rocks fringed the road, which turned suddenly to the right to skirt a broad bay, where the town of Millport began. Sandstone villas bordered the road on one side only; across the bay the small painted houses and shops stood out brightly.

The tide was out, leaving a good stretch of smooth wet

sand from east to west, an inviting short cut. Matthias had leapt athletically over the promenade rail. Taking off his trainers and socks, he ran across Kames Bay, savouring the difference between road running and running on sand. Going home with slightly sandy feet was a price worth paying. At the other side he checked his running time on his stopwatch, sat on the rocks to dry off his feet and headed for the metropolis.

When they arrived at the pub, Dean and Connor joined him, while Graziella and Markus took another table with Kathryn. Alice had headed straight to the bar to place her order.

"If only he hadn't such a damned air of entitlement." Dean cast a darkly brooding glance at Paul Aitken, who was standing at the bar with Hughes and O'Flaherty. Beside him, Connor Crozier sighed theatrically, anticipating a version of Dean's usual diatribe.

"Look what he's studying - History of Art at St Andrews, all part of the Kate and William syndrome. All the posh people are flooding there to reflect in the vicarious glamour. He's not even studying archaeology so he's keeping someone serious out of a place in this dig. Told me he'd chosen the course as he thought he'd better keep up to date on the family heirlooms."

It was too easy to wind Dean up, Connor thought, which made him an ideal target for Paul's baiting. In fairness, studying archaeology had not been a requirement for selection. Still there was no point in challenging Dean in his present mood.

"Are you jealous?"

"Ha, I'd back Scottish education against any public school, even though no-one put chocolates on my pillow at night. It's true," he protested at Connor's sceptical look. "They do it at Harrow. I saw it in a documentary. Still," he conceded, "his polished confidence lures the birds. Aye and then the trap is sprung, like Bruegel's *Winter Landscape*."

All right he knew he was name dropping, but Dean wanted to show his state education didn't preclude aesthetic taste. "Paul doesn't care about any of his conquests. They're just trophies to him."

"You only care about one, though." Connor had already noted Dean's behaviour towards Alice, a mixture of shyness and bravado. "But I wouldn't advise you to refer to her as a bird in her hearing, or I predict you'll be flattened like the birds in your painting."

Despite himself, Dean grinned. "Aye, but I'll not stand by while Alice falls for him," he muttered. Dean was disappointed that, after what he considered a promising start to a deeper relationship, Alice had seemed happier to slip back into being equally friendly with everyone, rather than responding to his readiness to take their friendship a stage further.

Another pint?" Dean stood up and made his way to the bar, neatly shouldering Paul aside to signal his order to Martin McCrone.

Incredibly the tactic worked. Dean turned to Alice. "I'd offer to buy you a drink if I didn't know that I'd be likely to have my head bitten off. Are you happy standing at the bar? Connor and I are at the table over there."

When they made their way across, Connor suddenly found that he had to consult Fraser about the programme for Wednesday. "I had wanted to ask you about your university research," Connor said as he rose to go.

"Tell us instead," said Dean, as Alice took her seat opposite himself and Matthias.

Alice was the only one on the course who had any expertise in the period being investigated and was passionate about the subject.

"If I am accepted into the Masters course, I want to research the position of women in Norse society," she told them. "So much of history centres around what the men were doing and I agree with those who argue it's time to redress the balance. I want to find those women who have been recorded as taking significant action, perhaps as regents for their minor children, their problems and their effectiveness. And how they were regarded by their contemporaries. I have a few ideas but I haven't fixed on any particular woman. The case of Queen Margarete of

Norway at the end of the twelfth century is a definite possibility. She played a significant part as a mediator in a bitter dispute over who should be appointed as the Bishop of Stavanger. Later, her enemies alleged that the widowed queen had poisoned her stepson, the new King Haakon. I am particularly interested that she fits into a stereotype in the long history of women accused of being poisoners."

Dean gazed at her enthralled. He could not have passed a spot test on what she had just said, but he could write a sonnet on her eyes.

When time was called at the pub, it was still light; in Scotland the days were longer than further south.

"The night is young," Connor said, as they exchanged the warmth of the pub for the fresh sea breeze. "Do you think that water is too cold for a swim?"

The suggestion got a mixed response.

"Depends," Markus was genuinely unsure. "They say sea water is warmer at night than during the day, but I have absolutely no idea if it's true. Once you are in and swimming strongly, it should be fine."

"The problem is the temperature when you come out," objected Graziella, with a mock shiver. Still," Her voice tapered off; she was obviously tempted.

"Let's shelve it for tonight and pencil it in as a '*definite maybe*' for later in the week." Alice wheeled her bicycle into the road. She glanced at Matthias, the only one without wheeled transport.

"Do you think you can beat us home?" she challenged.

"Perhaps not all the way, but I could probably beat you to the end of Kames Bay. The tide is out so I can cut right across. Ready?"

At Alice's nod he took off at a smart pace, while Alice started to peddle as fast as she could out of the town, past the sandy stretch of Kames Bay. By the time she rounded the bay she saw Matthias was correct in his forecast and was running steadily well ahead of her. Kathryn and Paul, on their own much speedier bikes, were already gaining rapidly on him and passed him with a carillon of bells. Alice herself passed him at the Lion Rock.

The mood that night at the hostel was cheerful; the students had different characters and enthusiasms, but some of the tensions had eased and there was a general atmosphere of toleration and companionship. Alice went to sleep happy and looking forward to the coming days.

BERGEN 1263

Harald could not pin-point when his feelings for Ragnhild began to change. But he knew to the day when he had realised that he loved her. He knew the year, the month, the day, the hour, the minute.

Love had been in the air. Haakonshalle was being prepared for a wedding feast in 1261. Haakon Haakonson, known as Haakon Unge, the Young to distinguish him from his father, was to marry Rikista Birginsdottir. Harald had been perched on a rock above the town in the throes of composition, searching for the words to describe a young woman, the idealised lover in his poem. Her eyes would not be blue, but blue-grey; they would change colour; when she wore blue they would take on a bluer hue, when she was garbed in green, her eyes would mirror that colour; grey one day, blue another.

Suddenly he realised he was thinking of Ragnhild, no woman yet, but a child no longer. He looked at the clump of sea thrift nestling among the rocks, the petals delicate, but tough, the foliage greenish-grey, a slash of bright colour among the dark rocks. This morning as she darted around the hall, absorbed in the preparation of garlands, Ragnhild had been wearing a simple light grey gown and her eyes had sparkled with that colour.

That day, Haakon the younger's bride was beautiful, with ash blonde hair and eyes of palest blue. But Harald's ideal had more vivacity. In his song, the bride would have Ragnhild's eyes, her lips, her smile.

CUMBRAE 2005

By the third day of the project they had settled into a regular rhythm. Morning briefing, hard physical work at the dig, research and writing up their log books, and a fragment of social life in what time remained. The students' rota was arranged so that they worked in teams, but these changed slightly each time, so that they worked with different members of the group.

The work was repetitive and although the broken tuning peg had provided key evidence of medieval activity at the site, there was nothing that marked it as specifically Norse. It could have come from any country and it could have been thrown away by a Scottish musician. Their initial delight at the discovery had waned, but interest soared again when O'Flaherty dropped the idea of a hoard of treasure into that morning's briefing.

"I thought that would wake you," he smirked. "Genuine archaeologists are just as interested in coprolite, but gold and jewels get everyone's blood coursing. First and foremost, this is no fictional treasure. On his voyage to the Firth of Clyde Haakon called in at Orkney and the Western Isles, sent ships to raid the north of Scotland, collected tribute, taxes, gifts and to some extent plunder. One of his ships was specially assigned to carry it. And this very ship got into dire difficulties somewhere in the little stretch of sea that you passed on your way up here."

Not surprisingly, the sieved soil was examined carefully

that day, but if any of Haakon's treasure had found its way to this spot on Cumbrae it was deeper than that morning's excavation reached.

By common agreement the team stopped for the day after the lunch break. That evening Connor and Fraser McCrone were planning to present their first Irish music night at *The Crocodile Rock* and Connor wanted to squeeze a final rehearsal of the group. Alice had offered a few suggestions for songs. She was no musician, but she knew the words and was happy to join in any communal singing.

Now Dean knelt under the fly sheet that had been pitched over the site of the main cutting. He was alone. The others had already set off for Millport. Tonight was just to be an impromptu musical performance, a trial run through for a more ambitious event on Friday, but Connor had high standards. His enthusiasm had succeeded in extracting promises of participation from Markus and Graziella. Even Professor Hughes had promised to bring along his banjo, if O'Flaherty brought his tin whistle.

Dean had no desire to accompany them. His mood was low; he was bitterly disappointed. Alice had not looked at him once that day, nor deigned to throw a single word in his direction. Paul had constantly thrust himself into the limelight, flattering and flirting, deliberately trying to antagonise him. Dean recognised this but was unable to shrug it off, or prevent himself sinking into deeper despondency. He had tried jocular flattery on Alice, but with a distinct lack of success.

"Wow, the sun has come up," he had said, as Alice had arrived for breakfast that morning. She did not respond as he had hoped, but instead looked rather disconcerted at the remark.

And now he was alone, wallowing in self-pity and rising resentment. Why could this snobbish interloper not stay in his own midden? If only Paul had gone to Egypt. He could have afforded it. He was also someone Dean could happily imagine in an Egyptian sarcophagus. In fairness, Paul's teasing was just as much directed towards Alice herself, just to see if he could provoke a response from her. But Dean was in no mood to be fair.

Irritated, Dean started to remove a small brown pebble out of the earth. Just another insignificant item. They had already removed the soil to a significant depth and carefully, scoop by scoop, they had sieved it, so nothing would escape them. He decided to finish the last few centimetres of the peaty earth and then call it a day. Dean thought it strange to find even a single pebble, for the rest of the earth was the purest peat. Properly dug and dried it would have made splendid fuel. But the whole of the Isle of Cumbrae was a natural heritage site. After the dig was finished the site must be filled back in, the whole area restored to its original condition.

Dean probed and scratched around the pebble but it just wouldn't come loose. It stuck fast and was in any case far longer than he had first thought. Longer? Dean took a small trowel and tried to dig the damned pebble out. When he had excavated about one centimetre, however, he carelessly gouged along the stone. In doing so he unearthed a leathery piece of cloth from the brown chunks. This was no pebble, but clearly a human toe, now exposed amidst the rotting fragments of a shoe!

In sheer shock Dean stumbled backwards into the upright pole of the tent, which bent under his weight and broke over him. This could not be part of a Viking burial or Viking treasure. This was a corpse, and one that certainly did not date from the thirteenth century.

Partly horrified at his grisly discovery and partly as excited as a young bloodhound, Dean wormed his way out from under the canvas of the collapsed tent, aiming to cycle to Millport and tell the others in *The Crocodile Rock* the news. The police would have to be informed, but he was not sure what effect dialling 999 would have on an island that as far as he knew had only one police officer. It would probably go to a call centre somewhere on the mainland. He rose to his feet gingerly, trying to estimate where it was safe to put his feet.

"Can I help you?" A man in a seaman's cap had appeared from the direction of the ferry. He was wearing the insignia of the ferry company on his sweat shirt. "What has happened? Are you hurt?"

"No, no. It's all right," Dean stammered. For some reason he did not want to divulge what he had just found to a stranger.

"I saw your tent had collapsed on top of you and I just thought you could do with some help." Tom Forrest threw the young student a bemused look, that was less than friendly. He was tolerant of the families who descended on the island each summer to make sandcastles on the beach, hire bikes and boats and give the island's economy a much needed boost. But he was much less tolerant of other attempts to make money by exploiting the island's resources. As for this delay to the road-works, he considered it a piece of nonsense. He had no time for these city-dwellers with their little paint brushes, miniature trowels and spatulas. Kindergarten toys. And now this clumsy oaf couldn't even keep a tent up. Yes, they might have book-learning, but they were no use to man or beast in the real world.

Dean quickly extricated himself from the collapsed tent, bedecked with the vital map of the dig site. He muttered something incoherent to Tom. With one pull he freed his bike from the undergrowth where he had parked it only three hours before and raced at top speed along the closed section of the road, as if fleeing from a ferocious manhunt.

Tom watched the disappearing figure. "What's wrong with him?" He shook his head. "First he wrecks the tent, then he just pushes off?" Tom took off his cap and ran his fingers through his tousled hair.

"Ach, do I need to understand it?" He looked at his watch, Two fifteen. Time to get going. The next boatload of tourists awaited. As he made his way back to the ferry, the sun broke through the clouds and spread a chain of a thousand diamonds on the surface of the water. The flag on his ship fluttered in the west wind. In his youth he had sailed the seas and oceans of the world, but not for one minute did he regret returning to the island of his birth.

Breathing deeply, Dean rode in the direction of Millport.

He still shuddered every time he thought of that bone. Suddenly he felt stupid. What if it hadn't been a human bone but something else? Maybe from some animal or other. No, he was far enough on in his archaeology course to be able to distinguish human bones from animal ones. It was definitely a segment of a toe.

When he reached *The Crocodile Rock*, he saw through eyelashes damp with sweat a group at the edge of the pavement. Alice and Paul were standing with another couple of students. Smoke rose from a cigarette in Paul's right hand. The other lay lightly but possessively along the wall, almost touching Alice's shoulder, but not quite, before edging closer. When her look met Dean's, she shook Paul's hand vigorously from her shoulder and drew away from him. Dean noted how she rolled her eyes upwards.

Then he hit the wall.

He was up and inside the pub before either Alice or Paul could react. When he opened the pub door, the place was in semi-darkness, the blinds drawn to enhance the effect of the flashing disco light. Blinded, he stumbled over the threshold and peered across the room. Slowly his eyes got used to the dim light. This was meant to be a rehearsal but Martyn had put out a board advertising, "Ceilidh today, musicians welcome." Normally the pub filled up towards evening, but today the good weather had attracted a crowd of day-trippers. It was his son's idea, but he had to admit that it had succeeded in attracting a good crowd. The music could scarcely be heard, however, over the noise of the customers.

Dean pushed his way ruthlessly through the throng of sweating bodies.

He skirted the snooker table, narrowly avoiding a player's elbow as he lined up his cue for a shot. When he spotted Alan Hughes, he was right at the back under the skeleton of a gigantic basking shark, in the middle of a group of musicians. O'Flaherty, blowing blithely on his tin whistle, was perched on a stool beside Graziella who had been given a quick course on playing bodhran and was now drumming enthusiastically in time to the lively tune. Markus was holding a borrowed fiddle, listening, bow lowered, to the tune. Connor had put aside his banjo and was playing uilleann pipes, all the while guarding against the danger of the long neck of Hughes' banjo knocking off his specs.

Despite the urgency, Dean shrank from the idea of appearing centre stage to break his news, or taking any action that would silence the music and draw everyone's attention to him.

Hughes spotted Dean, however, and noted his scarlet face and panicked expression. When their eyes met, Dean gestured with a nod towards the door. Alan gave a brief answering nod, but played on to the end of the verse before stepping down as unobtrusively as possible and heading out.

Dean was waiting beside his bike, which seemed to have been tough enough to withstand its brief collision. The sun had now reappeared from behind the clouds but a light drizzle of rain had started to fall. There was no sign of Alice or any of the others.

The door of *the Crocodile Rock* opened and Alan emerged. Dean inhaled deeply. Where before he had been hot from his frantic bike ride, now he felt cold and shaky.

"Thank goodness for a breath of fresh air," Alan said as the pub door shut behind him and the noise subsided. Then he looked at Dean's ashen face. "What's wrong?" When Dean started to explain that he had found a shoe-clad foot. Alan raised a quizzical eyebrow – the very effect that Dean had been trying to emulate for days.

"That's not so surprising. If you want to make it as an archaeologist you'll have to get used to that kind of find, and sometimes even more grisly discoveries."

"You don't understand. It's not an ancient bone. It's modern. The shoe is like a summer sandal. And I think it's attached to a full body, although I didn't want to disturb it further."

Hughes looked at him in astonishment. "A modern sandal?" Footwear like sandals had been in use since antiquity. In some ways the designs had changed little. To avoid looking like an idiot, before raising any kind of alarm he would have to check Dean's story. Saying nothing to the others, they both swung onto their rain-soaked saddles and set off back to the site.

Susan Clearsmith grasped the sides of her kneeling pad and hoisted herself upright. She glanced briefly at the newly weeded part of her rockery. The south side of the garden was steep, practically precipitous, and needed constant care. Not for a moment though did she regret exchanging her house and garden in the leafy Pollokshields area of Glasgow for this villa perched on a hill above the town of Millport on the Isle of Cumbrae. From where she stood she had a clear view of the promenade, the beach, and beyond that of the two Eilleans in the bay where seals basked in the sunlight.

For most of her working life she had worked as a photographer and for the last two decades before her early retirement she had been attached to the Strathclyde Murder Squad as a forensic photographer. At that time her little room and kitchen on Cumbrae had been an ideal weekend bolt-hole. It had been in the family since she was a child and she had many happy memories of the annual family holidays they had spent there. Now she had reversed the pattern. She still had a small-pied-à-terre flat in Glasgow's Merchant City, but home was a large sandstone villa on Bute Terrace, overlooking Millport Bay. At first, when she cut down her commitment to her forensic photography job, she had commuted by ferry to Glasgow. She even claimed the journey was not much longer than the slow traffic-snarled route from her suburban Glasgow home to the city centre. Now that she was fully retired, she sometimes worked as a consultant, but this work had dwindled. The quality of mobile phone cameras meant that it was within the capacity of ordinary police personnel to record scenes of crime.

The mobile phone started to ring in her pocket, the vibration a snake in the Garden of Eden. Susan would have preferred seclusion, freedom from the constant pressure to 'be in touch' that was increasingly demanded in these times of slavery to electronic devices. When she worked full time she had been used to having to carry a pager device, which alerted her to ring police headquarters to find out why she was urgently needed. How clunky that now seemed. A single press of a button and she was connected to the world. Miraculous - but intensely irritating.

She removed her gardening gloves and dropped them into her trug. The phone rang on insistently till she pressed the accept call button. She already knew the caller was Dai Evans, the Detective Superintendent in charge of murder investigations. "Yes," she said tersely.

"Not taking you away from the hectic whirl of social life on Cumbrae?" Evans never missed an opportunity to tease her about her decision to move 'off shore' as he called it.

"Just ridding the garden of some ground elder. What's on your, for want of a better expression, mind?"

Dai refused the challenge. "Got your bike handy?"

"Of course." Susan's voice became businesslike. There was a well-rehearsed procedure when she was called to the mainland to a scene of crime. "Will a car meet my ferry in Largs?"

"No need darling." Dai added the endearment provocatively, trusting to the safety of the forty-mile distance separating them. This time we have brought you a convenient corpse, suspected murder victim, handily located on your beloved Isle of Cumbrae, half way between Millport and the ferry terminal."

"Is this a wind-up?"

"I never joke about murder." It was true. All sign of levity had vanished from his voice. "If you can start out, I'll get some facts together and email them to you. There will be no problem finding the site. The local PC is already there with the incident tape, but you'll also see tents."

"Tents up already? That's quick. We only have one policeman on the island, normally - unless he got the Boy Scouts on bob-a-job to pitch them."

"As I understand it, the corpse is on the site of an archaeological dig. The tents are theirs, but we'll be locking down the dig. Am I right in assuming you're on your way?"

"Yes," said Susan succinctly, as she swung lithely into the saddle. "I'll ring when I get there." Tossing her phone into her bicycle basket, she went freewheeling down the brae to join the outer circle road towards the ferry terminal.

Susan stood well back from the grave as the Forensic Services team began their careful uncovering of the corpse. Her zoom lens would give flawless close-ups of each stage of the operation. One finger that intruded pathetically was ringless. But, when the hand was revealed, a dark band was clearly visible. Cleaned up it might provide a clue to the identity of the victim. Susan sighed and prepared herself for a long shift. Despite years of grisly encounters with the victims of violence she had never become hardened. She had developed a protective carapace, but never forgot the once living human being.

As she looked round at the archaeological set-up it was hard to link it with the more well-known discoveries of Tutankhamun or Thebes. No attempt had been made to wrap this corpse or provide this young woman with valuable grave goods.

When the earth was removed from the upper body, although the clothing was rotted, the outline of a sleeveless blouse could be seen, so classical in design as to be from any potential decade of the late twentieth century, except that it would be summer wear. This was strengthened when a skirt was revealed, which barely covered the tops of the legs.

"Looks like a mini skirt," Dai Evans said. "That should give us an idea of when she was buried. I remember we did a project in school about the 60s. I had to take in old photographs of my mum. Almost indecent her dress was, in a swirly pattern you wouldn't choose for curtains."

Susan pressed and released the shutter automatically, but nerves had tightened her stomach like bicycle clips. The noise of the forensic team faded in volume, as if she were going to faint.

"Mind you," Dai continued, "that was nothing compared to what my father wore. His gear was still in the wardrobe, flare trousers and, believe it or not, platform shoes in psychedelic colours. Talk about…"

"Can we take a break?" Susan interrupted. The world had started to spin round and round. "I could do with a seat."

"No problem. We're more or less halfway through."

In the gazebo the team unpacked vacuum flasks and unwrapped biscuits. Susan unscrewed a bottle of water she had filled at the nearby Wishing Well, a spring of pure water that was a favourite stopping place for walkers and cyclists. The external world had stopped spinning, but her inner thoughts were chaotic and disturbed.

Dai was starting to come to terms with the case in his usual way, verbalising the known facts and marshalling theories and conjectures. "The problem with identification is that thousands visit Cumbrae in the summer months, and well into autumn. My dad came camping every July with the Boys Brigade pipe band." Dai always found the investigative challenge exciting. "Day trippers, cyclists, folk who rent houses and caravans – it's quite possible neither the victim nor the perpetrator had anything but a brief connection with the island."

"I think I can save you the trouble." Susan interrupted. She cleared her throat nervously. "I am pretty sure I know who it is."

After Alan had verified Dean's original find he had produced a mobile phone. The number of the local police station in Millport was posted beside the telephone in the hostel and he was glad he had entered it into his contact list, judging it better to ring there rather make an emergency 999 call. Shortly thereafter the sound of a motor bike was heard. Andrew MacGillivray, the sole police officer on the island, made short work of the uneven surface of the road as he sped to the spot. Within minutes of his arrival he had initiated the standard procedure for such a discovery and Strathclyde Police Headquarters in Glasgow had been alerted, statements from Dean and Alan had been taken down in his notebook and Andrew had begun sealing off the area with official incident tape.

When they got back to *The Crocodile* Rock the rehearsal had finished and the students had dispersed, unaware of the dramatic turn of events that would affect all of them, but O'Flaherty was still at the bar. It was clear that the project leaders had to discuss contingency plans and Dean decided he should leave them to it.

"Are you sure? You have just had a major shock." Alan would have been happier if he could have seen the lad join the others, but he could hardly say that he would accompany him till he found them. Dean was adamant that he could cope and headed off in the direction of the old pier right in the heart of Millport.

It was astonishing how many people were taking advantage of the sunny spell to stroll along the seafront: people playing crazy golf; older women sitting on the benches chatting and knitting; a few people on the beach. The school holidays had finished so most of the visitors were *'senior citizens'* some of whom had been applauding the music in the pub not that long ago.

Alice and Paul were nowhere to be seen. Perhaps they were in the café, Dean thought, making his way in that direction. In this he was partly right. Led by Graziella, most of the group had adjourned to the Ritz Café that proudly displayed an article from a popular Scottish newspaper, *The Sunday Post,* describing its ice cream as *'the best in Scotland.'* At that moment they were sampling the menu that had altered little in decades: *oysters, double nougats, 99s, McCallums, snowball ices.* When Dean spotted them through the large window they were just being served, and their choices had been wide-ranging. Most intrepid had been Markus, who had been unable to resist a modestly priced dish described simply as *Hot Peas* and had been brought exactly that, a dish of cooked marrowfat peas, served with vinegar, salt and pepper. The others had chosen ice creams but had to admit the smell of the peas with vinegar was enticing.

"Where on earth have you been?" Connor moved along to make room for Dean at the 50s style Formica tables, with their patterns of red and yellow coloured triangles. "I saw you for a moment while we were playing and then you disappeared. Surely our playing was not that bad?"

A quick glance round had shown Dean that Alice was not there, but Paul was. He could tell her about it afterwards, Dean thought, as he embarked on his account of the last traumatic few hours. His graphic account of the discovery changed the atmosphere from joviality to horror. Their experience of death was limited, mostly funerals of older relatives, with all the customary rites that society used to help mourners accept the inevitability of mortality.

One result of the questions and answers that followed was that Millport learnt of the news before any official announcements. Back to back with the students' tables were two seats occupied by locals. The word spread with such impressive rapidity that when Andrew MacGillivray returned to the Police Station it was to be greeted by a well-informed dog-walker. "I hear you've found a body round the back of the island. Do you know who it is?" Andrew was very much on his dignity in his role as the upholder of law and order on Cumbrae, rather than the trainer of the school football team and the young male in the Dramatic Society. His questioner, Sandy Gordon, had already reported his scoop to *The Largs and Millport Weekly News* and he didn't really expect Andrew to leak details, but it was worth trying.

Although, as a forensic photographer, Susan had been in many police stations in the West of Scotland, this was the first time she had sat on the other side of the table to give a statement in a murder inquiry. While MacGillivray readied the tape recorder and made the factual introductions, she silently marshalled the information she ought to pass on. The young police constable waited patiently. For most of the year he was the sole police constable on Cumbrae and this was his first big case. He had met Susan Clearsmith socially, but now she was here as a vital witness. He wanted to do everything properly.

"I believe the body is that of Elinor Sommers," she began, trying to speak dispassionately, despite her internal turmoil. I don't remember the exact date she disappeared but it'll be easy to check..." Her voice continued automatically but her mind raced ahead to the day Elinor had disappeared. The day the library did not open.

"At first no one noticed. The public library only opened on certain days and at certain times. Its stock was limited. Many local readers and visitors used the private library operated by the gift shop instead, where a wall of bookshelves held popular crime, historical and romance fiction, ideal holiday reading that could be borrowed for a modest sum, part fee and part deposit, which was redeemed when the book was returned."

She stopped short, aware that she was rambling, but so many memories were intervening and preventing her from making a succinct coherent statement. Sensing her confusion, Andrew hastened to reassure her.

"Just put in everything. At this stage we don't know what will turn out to be relevant."

"The town library was used mainly by residents," Susan continued, "but there was not enough work to occupy Elinor full-time. The bulk of her secretarial work was town administration, typing minutes of meetings or envelopes for the rates demands. When she was asked about her job though, she took pride in her role as the Town Librarian and she voluntarily spent lunchtimes organising the books and planning events that would turn the library into the cultural and intellectual hub of the community." Susan shifted uncomfortably on the hard institutional chair of the interview room; she shivered suddenly and fumbled for a tissue to wipe the moisture from her brow.

"No one noticed. The people in the office upstairs assumed she was in the library. When the first customer, old Mrs Berriman, found the door locked, she assumed she had mistaken the day. But, as a few more potential customers arrived, eventually the truth dawned. A spare key was found and the door was opened. Elinor was not inside. There was no sign that she had been in that day, apart from a jacket hung neatly over a chair behind the issue desk."

Susan's narrative continued, as she recounted the commonly-held version of Elinor's disappearance. But in one important respect she was wrong. Elinor had not been at work at all that day.

CUMBRAE 1972

E linor had risen very early that morning. She had woken to the realisation that she didn't have to be at work until after lunchtime, when she would be staffing the library. This was a precious concession she had just negotiated, to compensate her for the evening openings that were being piloted for a trial period. Today was the first of her free mornings and she intended to make the best of it.

She swung her legs out of the bed and decided that a perfect way to spend the time was to walk over the hill to Fintry Bay, *'the Bay of Foes.'* She could enjoy the peace of a solitary leisurely ramble. Early morning was a magical time on Cumbrae. The weather was mild, as it had been the day before, so she didn't need the jacket she had forgotten when she had left work.

She saw no-one as she passed the farm, although there were sounds of activity; milking had started at four and was already over. She was glad it was dry, as the ground was often churned up by the cows' hoofs as they moved between the milking shed and the fields. Already back in the field, they looked at her with placid bovine curiosity as she swung by. It was too early for any golfers to be teeing off, so, as the path narrowed before descending to sea level, she looked west towards Bute. It was hard to imagine that peaceful strip of water full of Viking longboats, their sails billowing in the wind and their prows heading for the shore. Elinor imagined the feelings of the Cumbrae islanders seven hundred years before as they saw the vast fleet enter the Firth of Clyde. At this early hour the channel was free of shipping, although later in the morning there would be yachts, ferries and perhaps even the occasional submarine.

Ahead the view was obscured by the undergrowth that encroached on the path. Elinor wore no watch but she was confident that she still had time to get down to the shore, go back along the coast and open the library. Calmly she resumed her walk; she had completed the first stage of her final journey on earth, unobserved by anyone.

BERGEN 1263

As the adzes struck the wood, the stores of nails dimin-ished and the boats took shape. Only the best wood was selected, oak for the main construction, pine for the strakes, masts and oars, spruce roots to tie the frames to the planks, or deer sinews which were even stronger. Finally, the large steering oar was at-tached to the starboard side. Soon they were at the stage of fitting out and provisioning. Boathooks and broad-axes were counted, two or three hundred ells of wadmal per ship for mending sails, a large number of needles, a supply of thread and cord, spikes rivets, gouges and augers. These may have seemed too trivial for Haakon's attention, but they were all necessary for a successful expedition and Haakon was not good at leaving even the smallest detail to others.

Haakon had little time for Ragnhild now; he had captains to meet and his son Magnus to advise, although Magnus already had plenty of his own ideas about how Norway should be ruled. When Haakon finally did snatch a moment with Ragnhild, what he had to say dismayed her and decided her finally on the step she had already been contemplating.

"Don't worry about your future," he had said. "Remember Cecilia."

Ragnhild could not in fact remember Cecilia, but she knew her story. A daughter by Haakon's mistress, she had been married twice, each time to cement Haakon's relations, first with a rival for the throne, then as a widow she had wed her father's ally the King of the Isle of Man. She and her husband had drowned, as he took her from Norway to her new home.

"We will not be able to secure you an alliance such as Ce-

cilia made, God rest her soul. But there are plenty of ambitious jarls and even petty kings who will be only too pleased to marry a daughter of Haakon. You can look to the highest. When we return from Scotland we shall settle the affair."

Ragnhild was horrified. Although Harald was a favourite of her father, he did not hold lands or status prestigious enough to fall into the category Haakon was describing as a future son-in-law. They had already talked of seeking his blessing, but had rejected it as impractical. Harald wanted to be a minstrel, a profession that was revered, but not one that a prospective father-in-law would welcome. As they sat and dreamed, their vision of happiness was to travel, to seek adventures that Harald would weave into his songs and perform in many places and to many peoples. Even if their future was to be more prosaic, they wanted to be together. And this could never happen at the Norwegian court, with the consent of Haakon. Elopement seemed a more and more attractive option and now their plight had become urgent. If ever there was an opportune time to elope it was in the present flurry of activity as the fleet prepared to sail.

It was Ragnhild who came up with the audacious plan. Bjorgvin was their only confidant. When he heard their proposals he was both incredulous and amused.

"You are going to elope, by travelling with the fleet and letting fate choose a suitable place to jump ship? It is the first time I have heard of a maiden eloping accompanied by her father."

Bjorgvin and Harald were already on the muster role; how Ragnhild was to get on board a ship was more problematic and how she was to stay undiscovered was an even knottier challenge.

"Your help would be a boon, but we will understand if you do not feel you can say yes."

Once he had agreed to abet them in their flight, however, Bjorgvin flung himself heart and soul into the planning. In fact, most of the details were decided by Ragnhild and Bjorgvin, as Harald was soon in the throes of composing a song of farewell to his homeland. Ragnhild already had some ideas about the flight and Bjorgvin made a good sounding board.

"I can't see how you are going to hide on board whichever ship you choose."

"But I have no intention of hiding, apart from my clothes. I've thought it all out and there are so many people coming from different parts to join the fleet. If I just look as if I have every right to be there, I can pass unchallenged as general crew. I know enough about ships to be handy. No one will be expecting someone like me to be an elite oarsman. I'll just be a lowly menial, scarcely worth a glance."

As a first step, Ragnhild donned her disguise and made periodic appearances around the docks so that others became used to her going back and forth on humble tasks. In breeches and nondescript tunic, with her hair carefully bound up under a rough cap, she practised striding out in a more masculine way, enjoying the anonymity she rarely experienced in her daily life.

Harald and Bjorgvin knew the ship they were to join. Although they were young, not yet at their full adult strength, they were both strong and well-trained and would take their turn at the oars. They had the right to a sea chest that doubled as a bench, so, amongst his gear, which included his beloved gittern, carefully wrapped in linen and surrounded by soft fleece wool, Harald could secrete additional items for their flight. But Ragnhild had to plan her wardrobe with care. Although she must travel light she carefully opened seams and, wryly aware of her belated gratitude to her mother for ensuring she had this skill, she sewed concealed pockets into her garments, in which she placed a small collection of her dearest treasures, a pair of gold earrings that had been a gift from her father to her mother, a clasp for her cloak that Haakon had given her on her thirteenth birthday, a single string of beads that she had owned since a child, when she had been fascinated by its different coloured stones and jewels. Under the lining of the cloak she hid a stout plain dress of coarse hemp for the day when she would assume her feminine garb again, but most of her possessions she would abandon when she disembarked from the ship and embarked on the journey with Harald that would last a lifetime.

Leaving Bergen was an emotional moment for Ragnhild. As a child she had sailed with her father among the maze of small uninhabited islands just off the coast. She had admired his skill as he steered deftly through narrow channels, winding round the rocky islets, choosing one to make land. They would jump ashore and she would gather sprigs of juniper, choosing as tinder the dried twigs that remained on the bush, a trick he had taught her. Even in wet weather it was a way to collect dry firewood, a sure-fire way he would chuckle. The aromatic smoke mingled with the smell of freshly caught mackerel sank into the deepest recesses of her memory, a time when she was a happy child.

In all honesty she had many pearls of happy childhood memories strung like the beads of her favourite necklace, that nestled snug at the bottom of her leather pack. It was a costly piece as it was made up of glass and carnelian beads strung on silver. The beads had been brought back from voyages to far lands and appealed to her childhood self, not for their value or rarity, but because they were not uniform either in shape or size. Although glass and cornelian alternated roughly, they were not strung to a fixed pattern but rather as a child might choose, now two beads, now three, now round, now square; best of all, little circles of wire held separate charms, a small gold rectangle, a tiny ring of jade beads. She had loved to twist it round daily, to display each in turn. Some of her costlier trinkets she had left behind: she did not want to be considered a thief as well as a runaway, but this memento meant more to her than the sets of showy gold shoulder clasps used to fasten her cloaks.

To maintain her disguise as a young man, Ragnhild had to be constantly vigilant. Some things were obvious, but others more unexpected. It was hard to guard against the habits of a lifetime when you did not know that they were habits.

"Why do you flick at your neck like that? Can you see backward and are waving to those behind you?"

She had been puzzled at Bjorgvin's question. Then she caught herself in the involuntary movement that had attracted his attention. Accustomed since childhood to long hair, she auto-

matically flicked it up when donning a jacket or a cloak. Each time she now put her hands behind her neck in this habitual motion she felt a sense of loss, that her shortened locks no longer needed this attention, but she had not realised that the gesture had lingered, perhaps to betray her.

Her other steps to pass undetected centred on blending in so that, as far as possible, she went unnoticed. She kept her eyes down. She carried a coil of rope, an adze, any object that made others assume that she was engaged in legitimate business.

Sleep was less difficult than she had imagined. No one had a personal space; each was shared by those on different shifts. As the ship sped on through all the hours of the day, taking advantage of the long hours of daylight in the north, rowers threw themselves down in the most convenient place so there was always somewhere for her to get some rest.

When the cooks came round with thick stews, she sat whittling a piece of wood to make a peg or using a bone needle to mend a piece of sailcloth and her bowl was filled as a matter of course.

It took the fleet two days to reach the first of the Shetland Islands; Hyfaltland was an easy voyage in favourable weather, but she rejected it as a place to disembark. It was too near to be a safe refuge from her father's wrath.

ORKNEY 1263

"When King Haco lay in Ronaldsvo a great darkness drew over the sun, so that only a little ring was bright round the sun, and it continued so for some hours.

He had a favourable breeze, the weather was fair, the armament beautiful to behold."

Surla Torvaldson, Norwegian Account of Haco's Expedition against Scotland

Neither Bjorgvin nor Harald were assigned to Haakon's flagship, but Haakon had not forgotten the quartet of young men who had been under Magister William's instruction, trained using Haakon's book of advice for young men as a textbook. 'The King's Mirror' described various scenarios that they might meet in later life depending on what careers they chose, whether as a kingsman, warriors or a merchant. Magister William took them through these with the advice on behaviour and morals. He was a good teacher, spicing their activities with humour. Erik's grasp of numbers was so poor that they joked he did not know how many boards he needed to ski. But he was good-natured and took the teasing in good part and did not resent their chuckles when Magister William suggested he play the part of a trader having to set a price for his goods, or secure a bargain for goods he wanted to buy. It was just as well that Erik's father was a wealthy jarl, whose son was highly unlikely to become a merchant. The format of the book was lively, a dialogue between a king and his son, which lent itself to dramatic presentation and Magister William encouraged them to read the parts aloud, although they must always play the king as the fount of wisdom and the son as an earnest young man. The text was both poetic and erudite, with descriptions of geographical wonders and examples from bible stories; winds were described as real characters with personalities and motivations. As a musician, Harald was inspired by the lyrical passages and tried to compose tunes to accompany the colourful language, making his melodies rise and fall like the swell of the billows.

Harald and Bjorgvin, like so many of the younger men in the fleet, were trained as warriors, but as yet untested in battle. Although they had not always followed Haakon's advice to eschew drinking, gambling and suchlike pursuits, they truly enjoyed the physical activities that their king preferred to see.

When riding for pleasure, therefore, they had nonetheless taken care to sit firm in the saddle, heels lower than toes, thighs gripping tightly to the horse's flanks, training their left hand to grasp the bridle firmly while gripping the shield, leaving the right hand to direct a spear-thrust with all their bodily strength. They revelled in the archery, sling-shot and spear throwing contests and even the challenge trying to do these with their left rather than right hand, all helping them reach their physical peak, and honing them for battle. They knew that Haakon would look on their efforts with approval. But in truth they did it mostly for fun, not to impress.

◆ ◆ ◆

The quartet had already found favour with Haakon in Bergen, making them an obvious choice when Haakon wanted young men to help show invited visitors round his flagship during their time in Orkney. It was an exercise in public relations that could only be enhanced by the presence of four handsome young men, well dressed and polite. Naturally they were wearing their best; Haakon was exacting and prescriptive about appropriate dress. Short linen shirts under their finest coats, mantles falling from their shoulders, trousers, shoes and accoutrements in brown, green or red, bareheaded, hair and beards carefully trimmed. They had bathed and their upper lips were shaved; moustaches were out of *fashion, now almost exclusively limited to the older generation.*

When they appeared promptly before Haakon, mantles discarded outside the royal cabin, he nodded in approval at their erect bearing and the neatly executed bows. He asked keen questions about the ships to which they had been assigned and their readiness for action before setting out their duties in the next days.

"After the mass in the cathedral the people will make their way to the harbour. My karls will be on shore to control their passage to the ship. You will meet them as they board and take them round the main and the upper deck, although the wives will probably be satisfied with the main deck. If two of you guide each group, you will be able to split up but make sure everyone in a group leaves the ship together.

The next day, her disguise as a youth intact, Ragnhild sat on the quayside only minutes from the cathedral dedicated to the Orcadian St Magnus. She paused in her whittling as the four young men passed and made their way up the special broad gangway in place for the visitors. True to their pact Harald gave no sign of recognition, but the irrepressible Bjorgvin, last of the quartet, gave her a brief conspiratorial wink when he spotted her. She was, after all, wearing some of Bjorgvin's grubbiest clothes and most of her meagre wardrobe had come from Bjorgvin, whose shorter height made then a better fit than anything she could have found elsewhere. The others had teased him about his tendency to hold onto old clothes that they considered absolutely unwearable. The son of one of Haakon's richest jarls, Bjorgvin had just grinned.

"That's my fishing jerkin," he had protested when Erik held it up tauntingly, threatening to throw it out of the window. Even when selecting apparel for Ragnhild's disguise he had not given up that particular item.

"Perhaps it is as well," Harald had said, looking down at it contemptuously. "It's so scruffy only rich people could get away with wearing it. On a poor sailor lad, it would draw attention, as most beggars would have too much pride to be seen in that.

The quay was busy with people waiting to see Haakon and

the other prominent figures pass by. Mostly the crowd was made up of people from the fleet, curious to see the powerful personages who would determine their fate. The Kirkwall townspeople were less in evidence, choosing rather to go about their business with an air of irritation at this disruption of their daily lives.

Ragnhild waited patiently for what she knew would be the briefest of sights of her father. What she had heard of him in recent days concerned her. There were signs that all was not well with the expedition. Normally Haakon could impose his will by sheer force of personality. He was wise enough to seek the advice of his counsellors, but ultimately he had always wielded power. Now his main plan of attack had foundered. It was flattering that his captains refused to mount an attack down the east coast of Scotland without Haakon's leadership, but strategically this would have meant the Scots had to split their forces to meet the dual threat. Haakon was incensed that he had been thwarted. Where he should have been able to command, he was finding he had to compromise. She knew her father was capable of outburst of rage, though these had never been directed at her. Having to abandon key aspects of his plans had left him with a sense of outrage that he found hard to conceal.

When Haakon appeared, Ragnhild immediately stood up respectfully and, like the others on the quay, followed the progress of the king as he boarded his flagship. Haakon wore his most regal garb and exuded confidence, power and affability. Only his daughter saw beneath the façade to a mere mortal struggling to play a convincing part.

When the expedition finally left Orkney, the reality of Haakon's long reach was the major problem the lovers faced; it stretched from Orkney across to the northern coast of Scotland and to all of the Western Isles. It was something Ragnhild had known intellectually as she listened to discussions at the court. But when she saw the tributes loaded, signs from the petty kings of the western islands that they accepted Haakon's rule, she could not envisage that any of them would give them sanctuary and *allow them to live, however obscurely, in their land.*

The journey was lasting too long, she thought impatiently. The stays in each place seemed interminable. They had still been in Orkney in August, when the sun was covered by the moon and the world went dark for seconds. Some superstitious sailors were daunted by the eclipse, but Haakon dismissed any talk of ill-luck scathingly, encouraging waverers to think pragmatically. The sun had been dimmed for the Scots as well and could not be read as a sign of impending disaster for only one side.

CUMBRAE 2005

Eventually Susan finished her statement and emerged from the police station into the harsh realities of 2005. The recording would be transcribed and she would get the opportunity to read it before she signed it.

All the details had been general knowledge, ultimately reported in the local press as an unsolved mystery. Elinor could have gone out for a breath of fresh air and exercise, strolled out onto one of the nearby jetties. She had even been known to practise on the nearby tennis court. It was a fine day. Her usual clothes, short mini-skirt and knitted twinset, would have been warm enough without the jacket.

There was no sign of the small shoulder bag she took to work or her purse, so she had money. But no shopkeepers had served her, nor had any one noticed her on her way to work that morning. Although Elinor had disappeared, technically she was not even a missing person. She was over sixteen, an adult in Scots law, permitted to marry without parental consent, perfectly entitled to leave home if she decided to do so.

Opinion had been split. Elinor was an attractive girl with many friends, male and female. She had no steady boyfriend, but you never knew, said the more malicious gossips. Girls were devious; she could easily have had a romantic relationship that she kept secret. Surely though, even if she left no note, she would at least have made contact eventually to reassure her frantic mother that she was safe. It was uncharacteristic behaviour.

As the days went by the theories became wilder. The shops were hubs of speculation.

"If you ask me," Fiona, the local hairdresser had declared, as she deftly unwound rollers, brushed out curls and sprayed hair, "she's likely been abducted by white slave traders."

"Aye right," her companion said sceptically, stirring another spoonful of sugar into a weak coffee that would in later days be reinvented as a skinny latte, "and how would they have captured her in a street full of folk and got her onto the boat against her will?"

In 1972 the present pier used by the roll-on drive-off ferries that plied between Millport and Largs was not in operation. Foot passengers arrived at the old pier in the middle of the town; a large car ferry operated only once a week.

"They'd not have used a ferry. If you ask me she was taken off in one of them houseboats anchored in Newton Bay. She was aye on that jetty giving Tom Forrest the glad eye, the wee flirt. They could have snatched her from there and no one the wiser, all playing crazy golf or building sandcastles."

The gossip had continued. Some had looked askance at Tom Forrest. But the mystery was never solved. Gradually the newspapers carrying stories speculating on her fate were turned into wrappers for fish and chips. Life on the island had resumed its placid pace, a placidity that had now been shattered.

His shift on the Largs-Cumbrae ferry finished, Tom Forrest arrived in Millport to hear the explanation for the police incident tape he had seen on his way home. As he strode to his home in West Bay, past the jetty where his father had run the family business, he had encountered an excited group of locals outside the newsagents. The news on the street was far more dramatic than anything the daily papers contained. Belatedly Tom realised the brief part he had played in the unfolding drama. He had thought he was just witnessing a minor mishap, when he had spoken to that student; he now understood the lad who had made the discovery had been in a state of shock.

Needless to say Susan's journey out of town and her return to the police station had been observed and the town waited with impatience to learn more details of exactly what was wrong. Later, when the identity of the body became general knowledge, Tom was glad that the lad had not divulged the details of the discovery to him so that he could claim with honesty that he knew no more than the others.

Susan would certainly be the target of questions that she would probably not be at liberty to answer. He decided to ring her when he got home. In many respects he was her only true friend on the island. Although, since relocating to Cumbrae, she was on friendly terms with many folk, there was still the remnant of a quibble that she was not yet a local.

It was a relief for Susan to get back home from the police station and out into the garden. She was more shaken by her experience than she would have thought, but then nothing in her past encounters with death had prepared her to cope with a victim she had known so well. Tom's phone call, suggesting they meet later on, had been comforting.

Montmorency's ecstatic greeting had also been a comfort, well worth the treat she had tossed to him as she switched on the kettle and spooned some instant coffee into a mug. The little patio outside was narrow, just enough room for a small table and a few chairs before the steep slope. A former owner had built terraced beds to optimise the growing space and Susan had kept the feature, giving each bed its own distinctive character, plants specially to attract butterflies, towards the bottom blueberry and raspberry canes, netted to prevent the fruit providing gourmet meals for the garden birds.

Glancing towards them as she settled into a seat she sighed. Through the raspberry canes, a bald head could be seen and soon a blue pullover appeared. A figure emerged and started to climb up the garden steps. Susan rose and before the man had reached the top she had fetched another mug of coffee. "Hello, Sandy," she said. "Take a seat and I'll tell you what I can."

It was easier to take control of the situation. Susan knew

Sandy Gordon was just the forerunner in what would become a queue of acquaintances wanting the all latest news. He ranked high in the league table of local gossips and anything she told him would spread exponentially throughout the town, saving her from answering the same questions again and again. Similarly, she would be sure to learn quickly of any new snippets of opinion she hadn't yet heard.

Satisfied he had plenty to report to his cronies, Sandy took his leave at last and Susan slipped on Montmorency's lead to take him for a good walk, before heading off to meet Tom. Once past West Bay she could slip him off the leash and let him run free for a good romp through the rough grass.

While the others had gathered at the Ritz Café after the rehearsal, Alice had walked right through the town past the old pier and through the narrow street that led to West Bay. She did not plan to walk all the way round to Fintry, but, where the road turned north, there was a piece of rough ground with a bench looking over to Little Cumbrae and beyond that to Ailsa Craig, the rocky island known as *Paddy's Milestane,* as it marked the half way point between Scotland and Ireland.

It was a sea route that had been travelled for more than a thousand years, in all kinds of craft. By Haakon's time it was a regular shipping lane between the islands and Ireland. Before the Norsemen, Saint Columba and his monks had braved the waters in lightweight wicker coracles built of branches bent to shape and covered with skins to keep out the water. And women had made that journey too. Alice knew that Eithne, St Columba's mother, was said to have followed her son and lived till her death on Eileach-an-Naoimh, a tiny island six miles north of Mull. There were many reasons women could have embarked on voyages; to join husbands in a new land, to visit family like Eithne, to escape.

CUMBRAE 1263

Ragnhild strode through the camp with a purposeful air, skirting the groups of tents and carefully rounding the fires to the windward to avoid the smoke. Haakon's fleet had finally arrived in the Firth of Clyde and now there was a substantial force camped on the Isle of Cumbrae just opposite the town of Largs, while negotiations continued.

She had slung a bundle over her shoulder and, to a casual observer, she was going on an errand to collect or deliver something for her master. This ruse had stood her in good stead over the last months and she had developed other tactics to avoid arousing curiosity. She rarely stayed in conversation with any one person or group. Often, to move on, she would glance away quickly as if she had spotted someone and mutter that she must go. All the men had their own concerns and pastimes, as they awaited orders, and no one had any real interest in a scrubby youth.

She had made several such journeys outside the main encamped area, but this time she was leaving for good. Her baggage was already gone, stashed safely in a spot half way up the hill that rose above the camp. A track split off at an angle to the coast line, a route trodden down by the cattle that abounded on the island, as they were moved to different pastures. Now, as she took the inner route, she knew this marked a decision that would affect the rest of her life, choosing Harald above family and homeland. She had not been walking long, when she was joined by Harald and together they made their way to the spot he had chosen for their hiding place.

By the time the fleet reached the Firth of Clyde in September Ragnhild had known that for herself and Harald it was now or nothing. They would have to leave the fleet and find some place to live in Scotland, either for good or at least till they could travel on in search of a place they could make their home. After her father had imposed his will on the King of the Scots, the fleet would disperse, Haakon's allies to their own territories and the Norse ships back to her homeland, which she was resigned never to see again.

There was something different about the Isle of Cumbrae; it had no towering mountains or long beaches of dazzling white sand but it had a quiet air almost of domesticity, that attracted Ragnhild more strongly than the spectacular scenery of many of the islands they had passed on the journey south.

Haakon had forbidden plunder here and enjoined those of his men whom he gave permission to land to treat the islanders gently. They lived from the sea and the land, fishing in small boats, gathering shellfish, ploughing the soil, raising sheep and cattle. A small monastery of priests ministered to their spiritual and medical needs. When Haakon landed and set up camp, the islanders supplied milk, meat and mead without either protest or any overt sign of enthusiasm.

At last Ragnhild and Harald felt they had a found a place to live. It had been an easy matter to slip inland and make their way uphill to a small outcrop of rocks. It was a natural formation, but it could be incorporated into a basic dwelling, roofed with heather and bracken and made secure from wind and rain. There was little chance of discovery. All the interest of those Norsemen who had come ashore on the island was directed seawards. It was unnecessary to climb high to see across to the mainland where Alexander's force had gathered. The size of Haakon's fleet had become a drawback to efficient organisation: many were strangers to one another; few had any clear idea of who was meant to be where. This worked to the couple's advantage. Ragnhild could slip off unobserved, while Harald was free to continue as a member of the fleet, mingle with the others in the Norse encampment, fetch supplies for them to store and as often as possible to join Ragnhild in their makeshift abode.

Bjorgvin was often ashore and he reported glumly that the

truce negotiations seemed to have finally collapsed. No-one knew when, or even whether, Haakon would give the order to make a full scale attack. It seemed unlikely, now. The peace envoys reported that the Scots army was in good heart, well-trained and confident, many of them well-mounted. The country people also seemed loyal to their king, and hostile to the negotiators Haakon had sent. At an inland meeting in the town of Kilbirnie, the envoys had felt in such danger that they had broken off their talks. It looked as if war was inevitable.

CUMBRAE 2005

lice's thoughts were interrupted by a light touch on her left knee and she was brought back into the present by the soft panting of a small white dog, who had clearly selected her as a likely playmate. Once sure of her attention, he scampered off, stopping to look round to see if she was going to join in the game. A slim grey-haired woman holding a leash was approaching, smiling fondly at her dog's antics.

"Your poor little dog is lame. He's hurt his leg." Alice knelt down to pat Montmorency, who had raced back and was now licking Alice's hand, eternally expectant of a doggy treat. He was always happy to stop his romp to make friends with anyone who responded to his tail-wagging overtures.

"I used to think he was a fraud," Susan declared, looking at Alice indulgently, as she and the small dog played together. Susan was happy to be friendly with anyone who appreciated Montmorency. "For some reason, known only to himself, he has a habit of running on three paws and I thought the giveaway was that it wasn't always the same leg. But I've learned since that, although he looks quite happy, it does mean that he has a weakness in both legs." She bent to clip the leash back on the West Highland Terrier. "What is his name?" Alice had been promoted to trusted friend and graciously allowed to tickle his tummy. Tail wagging furiously, Montmorency was clearly not yet ready to take his leave of his newest playmate.

"He's Montmorency. But that's only for short. His full

Kennel Club name is Bishopton Montmorency of Belnahua. I wanted to call him Jock, but somehow that seemed disrespectful. Even as a twelve-week-old puppy he had an inflated sense of his own dignity."

"Sure it's a name that would grace an Irish wolfhound." Now that Montmorency had decided it was time to move on, Alice fell into step beside Susan.

"It's quite genuine. Kennels have their own unique name for their pedigree dogs, then the dog gets a name. The rest of his name comes from lists of fictional dogs and actual Scottish islands. It would make a good pub quiz. I take it you are one of the archaeologists here for the dig. I saw you in the pub the other evening."

"Archaeologist is too grand a term. Right now I'm just a student, but I do want to make archaeology my career. It fascinates me." Alice was only too pleased to talk about the future, rather than dwell on the gruesome discovery of the body of a girl not much younger than she was.

◆ ◆ ◆

"So it is Elinor?"

Later that evening Tom and Susan sat at a table in *The Crocodile Rock,* two at the table, wishing as they had in their youth that it could be three. Then it had been only a matter of time, as Elinor had not yet attained the age when she was allowed into pubs. Now it was clear that her young life had been cut short and that she had had no chance of reaching that milestone.

The lounge was fairly quiet at this time. The planned musical event had been cancelled, or at least postponed. No-one felt that a jovial concert was fitting that night. The news of the identity of the body cast a gloom like a funeral pall. The customers were mainly locals; the summer visitors tended to arrive later, after making the most of the sunshine and fresh air.

Susan nodded. "The dental records will confirm it, but

there's no doubt."

The police investigation had already started and, having accepted the provisional identification, Andrew was already preparing to investigate the circumstances of Elinor's disappearance. She saw no reason for withholding the information from Tom, when Andrew MacGillivray was already interviewing people who had known her.

Perhaps it was just as well that there were no relatives to identify the body. Her widowed mother was long-dead, never having had the comfort of what nowadays was called *closure.* Susan shuddered at her own memory of the discovery. She had been used to the sight of death, although she had never succumbed to the black humour some used to shield themselves from the grim reality of a once vibrant human, now bereft of the spirit that proclaimed them an individual. But this was someone she had known and liked, someone who had been an important part of her youth.

Tom reached out a comforting hand, grasping hers tentatively. He had no idea what to say. In their trio he had always been the taciturn one, not completely silent, but mostly content to listen to the girls' chatter. Although his red hair was now muted to a salt and pepper shade, he was still a handsome man, his strong jaw and good bone structure unaltered, though wrinkles round his eyes bore witness to a lifetime gazing seawards and to a quick sense of humour.

Their trio. It had often split two to one, but in different ways and different combinations, not just male and female: Tom and Elinor were locals, Susan the summer visitor; Tom and Susan the ambitious ones, heading for further education and careers; Elinor the school leaver, content to get a job and stay on the island; Susan and Elinor tennis doubles partners pitted against just Tom on the other side of the net. It was the classical remedy for conflict, two united against one, the alliances shifting, with emotions, personality and external circumstances. Most of the time though they had been friends, just three friends. And now they were two.

It was a sombre group that met in the common room of the hostel the morning after the discovery of Elinor's body. Susan's identification of Elinor Summers had spread through the island and a tight-lipped Mrs Macbeth had told them the details of her disappearance thirty years previously.

By common consent the students had not ventured back into Millport the previous evening, mainly contenting themselves with snooker, darts and television, wanting to discuss the find but never quite succeeding. Dean had forestalled any questions by saying bluntly that he didn't want to talk any more about the experience and the rest did not want to challenge this, although most of them felt he would be better to express his feelings rather than repress them.

It was Markus, who first put his feelings into words. "We know when we study medicine that we must examine cadavers to learn more about the human body, its functions and causes of death. But they have to be treated with respect. This is a young girl about our age who was given no dignity, just disposed of." The others had become used to his cheerful light-hearted approach to life, so his deep anger made a profound impact on them. Learning her name made it worse, as the person who had been Elinor began to take shape in their imagination.

When Hughes and O'Flaherty joined them, the two academics had already heard from the police and discussed the options open to them in the current situation.

"As you know the site has been closed while the police carry out their investigations. They have completed their recording of the location of the body. The remains have already been removed to Glasgow for full forensic examination, but the site is still being searched for other evidence. It's possible that we'll be able to resume in a few days, when the police have completed that part of their investigation, but we won't know for some time yet. We are aware, however, that many of you have travel arrangements based on the assumption that you would spend at least ten days on this island and in fact that completion of this course forms part of your academic plans. For that reason, we intend to give you the option of staying on with an altered programme. We'll also understand if anyone wishes to leave."

"Think about it." Seamus had abandoned his normally jocular air and looked stressed and worried. "We'll answer any questions and you can count on our help, no matter what decision you take."

Soon it became clear that the majority of the group preferred to remain. Only Kenneth Matthews and Henry Percy left, Kenneth opting to rejoin his wife and grandchildren in the lodge they had hired in the Scottish borders, while Henry explained in a rather shamefaced way that he had an anxious mother to reassure. She had seen the media coverage and concluded that the whole population of Cumbrae, including her son, was in danger of being slaughtered by a homicidal maniac.

"She's never been in Scotland and her ideas are influenced by *Outlander and Braveheart,* but I'll have to get back home." This was almost the longest sentence they had heard Henry utter. Till now he had been almost reclusive, tending to retreat to his room in any free time and rejecting any suggestions to join the others at *The Crocodile Rock*. Within a few hours he was packed and on the ferry at the start of his journey home to Bradford.

"Until now, I've always been a bit hurt at how easily my parents can do without my company," observed Paul thoughtfully to Dean, who happened to be nearest him as the girls waved Henry off at the other window. "Maybe I should be grateful."

Now that Paul's pursuit of Alice had cooled, Dean's antagonism towards him had waned.

"I envy him."

"What?" Dean's head jerked up in surprise. Paul's default attitude was patronising and Dean's initial reaction was suspicion, but on this occasion Paul actually seemed to be sincere.

"I applied for this course because I just didn't want to go home. It's no fun being dragged around the county as a trophy son, expected to show up at every local event - *you must be nice to Mrs Trelawney at the church bazaar, darling. She's a perfect nuisance, but she practically runs the village. And the vicar will expect you to read the lesson on Sunday.*" Paul's voice held no affection as he mimicked his mother.

Dean's first instinct was to point out the pettiness of the complaint, the real hardships some folk had to face, but he resisted, vaguely conscious of a deeper unhappiness that Paul normally kept concealed beneath a camouflage of self-assurance. Now that Kathryn had decided to befriend Paul, he was less insufferable, Dean found.

"Odd that Henry's namesake is one of Shakespeare's heroes. I don't think Hotspur would have let his mother rule the roost."

"Maybe not, but I wouldn't count on it." Dean grinned at Paul and the wry smile he got in return signalled a male bonding that hours ago he would have thought inconceivable.

It was the knowledge that Elinor had been about their own age that made the strongest impression on the group and they understood and shared the anger that Markus had expressed.

"What kind of person could have done such a thing?" Graziella's dark eyes shone with outrage.

"When you think about it, the murderer could be someone you have passed in the street or sat near in the cafe. They say most people are killed by someone they know. If that's true, the person could well still be living on the island." There was silence as they digested Connor's theory.

"If that's true, I'd like to help find out who it was. Is that too melodramatic?" Alice looked round the group uncertainly. She had spoken from a deep conviction, but some support would help bolster her resolve.

"There may be little we can do, but we could ask questions and see if we can smoke out a likely suspect." Dean spoke slowly, but his reply was sincere and not just motivated by a desire to please Alice. "You've met Mrs Clearsmith. Suppose you talk to her. Graziella can concentrate on the Scotto-Italian folk. We'll take the regulars at *The Crocodile Rock*."

"I'm game for that," Connor agreed. "We can draw lots for who interrogates Professor Hughes and Doc O'Flaherty. They were on the island that summer as student volunteers at the dig. That makes them suspects too."

◆ ◆ ◆

"The preliminary report from forensics is inconclusive." Dai Evans cast an approving glance at the incident board that Ken had started on the wall of the inner room of the police station. He had arrived back on the early morning ferry and was met by the complete Millport police force, namely Andrew MacGillivray, who had driven ahead of him on his motorcycle to the one-man police station at the western edge of the town. Used to the impersonality of police headquarters with its brutal architecture and utilitarian furniture, Dai found the interior of the police station redolent of a bygone age. There were few reception desks nowadays where the pen was not chained to the counter, rather than casually lying on a battered clipboard. Idly he opened the Lost and Found book and saw that the last entry was of a small canvas bag, containing an orange and a purse with a five pence piece, found by an eight-year-old child on the beach. This new case took the young police constable into quite different territory.

"The base of the skull is shattered and mixed with fragments of what is no doubt local sandstone, though that will have to be confirmed. Whether that happened post or ante mortem is unclear. Similarly, whether it happened as a result of a blow struck deliberately, or from the head striking a stone accidentally, is still an unanswered question. Maybe surprisingly, there is no evidence from DNA examination of the clothes of any sexual activity, although we can't rule out that as a motive for the killing, a pretty girl spurning an unwanted advance, an obsessed suitor determined no one else would have her, if he could not. One thing is certain though. The body didn't bury itself. That turns it into a crime. A crime where there's no chance of discovering the murder weapon." Detective Inspector Dai Evans exploded with exasperation. "The on-site examination found no sandstone rock, but her skull was fractured by a rock. A rock!" His voice rose as he gestured towards the seashore yards away from the police station. This place has thousands of rocks: big rocks, wee rocks; smooth rocks, rough rocks; plain rocks, coloured rocks; enough to defeat even my genius."

His colleagues in Glasgow were used to his rhetorical rodomontades, but Andrew MacGillivray was surprised by Evans' stream of Welsh invective, honed by years of attendance at chapel. "Unless forensic discover flakes of paint from that crocodile's teeth we're stymied. Even if we find flakes of gold, apparently the whole place is strewn with miniscule gold particles. You don't need to look for the end of a rainbow on the Isle of Cumbrae; you just need to go along the beach with a bucket and spade." Evans shook his head in despair.

"That was just a good headline-grabbing story," Andrew protested. "It's just wee black spots in the rocks that contain infinitesimal amounts of gold. You'd need a full coal-lorry to make a sequin." His point made, he changed back to the case. "We might be better looking at motives and suspects. If it *is* a thirty-year-old murder, though, I agree that there's no point in searching for a blood stained rock."

"You say suspicion fell on Tom Forrest at the time?"

"Purely on the strength of gossip. Although she could just have left home for her own reasons, most people found that hard to believe, especially as the conventional way off the island is by ferry. Unless she was in disguise, it's hardly credible that no eagle-eyed local spotted her board the ship. Tom Forrest though had access to a motor boat through the family business, and could easily have taken her across to the mainland if he were helping her. The more macabre explanations had him sailing out into the firth and casting her body overboard."

"But I don't think we can discount Susan Clearsmith. She could have been jealous of Elinor's friendship with Tom, a classic love triangle."

"And her shock at the discovery was just an act? Could be." Andrew sounded dubious. He thought her shock was absolutely genuine. You might be able to feign shock in what you say and even how you say it. But the white face, the clammy hands? He did not believe even the most practised deceiver could fake these."

"She could still be guilty. At this stage no one can be ruled out. Evans had known and worked with her for years but his personal feelings couldn't be allowed to prevent him from doing his job. He rose and added Susan's name to the Murder Board.

"Strictly speaking it isn't a cold case, because it was never an official case." Half an hour later Andrew stood back and laid down his marker pen. He looked with frustration at the spaces he had left on the board, the many question marks. Time of death? Last known contact? Young adult disappears from home on a small island. She could have just decided to seek the bright lights of London, to join the swinging seventies." He waited hopefully for the detective inspector to prompt him as to what the next steps were in this case, which didn't fit into the more usual categories."

"We want to find out more about the girl, in particular her last known contacts. It was only thirty odd years ago. She would only be fifty if she had lived. There must be plenty of folk still on the island who knew her."

"A door to door enquiry would be useless, given the number of holiday lets. I could run off some posters asking for anyone who knew her to come forward. The shops would be only too pleased to put them up in their windows. I can also approach some of the more obvious contacts personally. I am sure there will be a high level of co-operation."

"Great. If you become submerged, I can pull in some help

from the mainland to take statements and so on. I'll be based on the island for a few days and then I expect I'll be back and forth." Just as Evans was about to pick up the telephone from the front desk it rang.

"Yes, speaking. Thanks. No problem, I'll find it." He turned to Andrew. "HQ have booked me in to the hotel round the corner. I think I'll use that as a base at present. I've quite a few things to set up. We'd be falling over ourselves if we tried to share the space here. Actually we'll be nearer one another than many people under the same roof at Police Headquarters in Glasgow. I'll leave you to it for now. Let's agree on a catch-up meeting at four this afternoon, unless you have anything urgent to report earlier."

Andrew lifted the hinge on the counter so that he could open the half door to let him into the area that led to the front door. Public information leaflets were pinned neatly on the wall board above two chairs. The lost and found ledger book lay on the desk, the most used record book. A panel with hooks for keys that had been handed in hung on the other side. Lost property was one of the main reasons people came to the station, particularly day trippers, frantic mothers who had mislaid purses, proud parents whose offspring had found a ring or a bracelet in the sand and were being taught their civic duty by handing it in. Children brought in their finds and left clutching slips that would allow them to claim the property if its owner had not retrieved it within a few months. All police stations offered this service but there was something about the circumstances of a seaside holiday resort that increased the occurrence; mothers and fathers packing and unpacking beach paraphernalia; bulging bags and stuffed pockets all led to items coming adrift. Idly Andrew thought of the archaeologists who were essentially also engaged in discovering items cast off or lost in a past age. This find, however, was unprecedented in the island's history.

The impromptu alternative programme saw the students assemble in the Museum of the Cumbraes, housed within the impressive Garrison House, built for the Revenue Officers who patrolled the west coast in the eighteenth century battle against smuggling. Known locally as *The Garrison,* it was almost as iconic as the crocodile rock and generations of children had been photographed on the low crenelated wall, which also provided a free fitness challenge as they ran along the wall either jumping the gaps or stepping up and down each notch.

All of the students had already spent some time there on the previous days' rotas, but this was a better opportunity to examine more carefully copies of old maps, articles in archaeological journals and local newspapers on previous discoveries on the island and photograph the fragments of the three Celtic crosses that had been found in the nineteenth century. There was a buzz of activity and by the mid-morning break they had undoubtedly achieved a much greater appreciation of the locality and its history.

"This place seems so timeless. What was it like in the 1970s?" It was an inspired question. Seated at a table with Hughes and O'Flaherty, Paul looked at Kathryn with admiration. Her gaze was innocent and her charm evoked an immediate positive response from the older men.

"Sure it was much as it is today. The music was different, often divisive." O'Flaherty looked at Alan for confirmation. The mods and the rockers fought pitched battles on the beach at Brighton. Each side had their own music. So did the Flower Power people, the hippies, the teeny boppers."

Kathryn said nothing and it was O'Flaherty who broke the silence. "I don't remember seeing any of that in Millport."

"The juke box in the Ritz cafe had most of the latest records," Alan added. "I remember you had long hair, tied in a ponytail. Mine wasn't as long as that, but my sideburns practically reached my chin."

Paul tucked his lips between his teeth. He was deeply uninterested in the hirsute history of two middle aged academics, but he was canny enough to suppress the comment on hairstyles that he desperately wanted to make.

"Did you make friends with any of the locals, sir?"

Unfortunately, his last word struck a jarring note. What would have been approved in many circles as good public school manners was anathema to O'Flaherty.

"The only locals I got to know well were the pubs." O'Flaherty stood up and produced his tobacco pouch and pipe. Even though the foursome were sitting in the outside courtyard of the Garrison cafe, the lack of ashtrays made it clear that smoking was not permitted. Without a word of further explanation, he strode away.

With O'Flaherty's departure the atmosphere improved and by the time the next session was due they had extracted a fair amount of information from Hughes. Alan had no recollection of the disappearance of Elinor, which had occurred just after the dig ended. He had made his way speedily back to Glasgow, as he had been keen to write up his findings as part of his Masters dissertation.

"Our conditions on Cumbrae were much more primitive than yours. We were camping and there were no modern conveniences like tables and chairs. We had to write up our notes sitting on a groundsheet and keep our books in waterproof bags. I doubt if Dr O'Flaherty had heard about the disappearance either. We left the island together and journeyed up to Glasgow." Alan felt it was natural, after the discovery of Elinor's body, that the young people should be curious and want to ask questions. He was embarrassed at O'Flaherty's curmudgeonly behaviour. His brusqueness had surprised him and he wanted to spare the youngsters another rebuff.

Through the window of the Ritz Cafe Susan could see Montmorency settle down with resignation. He was quite used to being hooked to the dog leash ring outside and seemed quite happy to be noticed and petted by passers-by, many of whom were obviously friends of long standing. As she waited for Alice to arrive, she stirred her first cappuccino thoughtfully.

Friendship and freedom. That was what her summer holidays in Millport had meant to the young Susan Clearwater. The only child of fairly elderly parents, she looked forward to her six weeks' school holidays with excitement and a degree of trepidation. Would she meet someone who would want to be her friend, at least for two weeks? Most families spent only a fortnight on the island; her family's purchase of a small flat meant that she and her mother could spend the whole of the school holidays in the cosy *'room and kitchen.'* They were joined by her father for his fortnight's holiday in July, and also each weekend, when he arrived on the Friday boat and left at the crack of dawn on Monday on the six o'clock ferry, to go straight to his work in Glasgow that morning.

She remembered the excitement of the departure at the start of their holiday: the taxi to Glasgow Central Station with its glass windows high above the concourse; the smell of the old fashioned steam trains; the individual compartments with windows that could be let down and secured by a strong leather strap. She remembered the lilac lupins on the railway embankments; the walk down the pier at Wemyss Bay to the waiting steamer; the exciting visit to the engine room to see the machinery that drove the paddles. She remembered the feeling of intense satisfaction of finding the large wicker hampers, which had been sent on in advance, sitting outside their Millport house, full of the clothes and linen they needed for the holiday.

As quickly as possible she had ventured out to reacquaint herself with the island's features, checking that nothing had changed, the shop selling home-made sweets, the sunken garden at the Garrison, with roses chosen for their strong smell as well as appearance.

Above all she looked for friends among visitors like herself, since most of the island children seemed to play among themselves or work in their parents' shops or cafes. She envied the family groups, where brothers and sisters were playmates.

When she reached her teens though, she found that over the years she had forged two friendships that lasted beyond each summer and endured year on year.

"You actually knew Elinor?" Alice had arrived promptly and was waiting for a Knickerbocker Glory, the realisation of a childhood longing, that she had recklessly ordered in place of the packed lunch resting untouched in her rucksack. The waitress set down a tall glass layered with Scottish strawberries, blueberries and Italian ice cream, and topped with raspberry sauce and cream, plenty to keep Alice occupied while Susan talked.

"Yes. We were *'summer friends.'* I can remember the day we first met. It was the end of July, the day of the exodus of the last of the Glasgow people, just before the Glasgow factories reopened. The next day the August people arrived, mostly folk from Paisley. I was expecting to have to wait till then to get some new tennis partners, but I strolled along to the public tennis courts anyway. In those days there were three hard courts at the front in the grounds of the Garrison. Elinor was there on her own; her usual partner hadn't turned up, but the court was booked so all she could do was practise her service. It only took me ten minutes to be back with my racquet and we played together for the rest of the summer. Later that day we learned that her usual tennis partner had been rushed to hospital in Glasgow with appendicitis. The Lady Margaret Hospital in Millport, just up the hill from the Cathedral of the Isles, had a small operating theatre but only for simple procedures. Elinor's friend was seriously ill, developing peritonitis and with a wound that needed dressing for weeks after she came home from hospital. Tennis was out for her for the rest of the month and so my partnership with Elinor became a fixture."

"How did you feel when Elinor disappeared?"

"It didn't make a deep impression on me at the time." Susan looked troubled. "Looking back at the dates I know I left the island the day after she was last seen. I was going to Italy and I was so excited, dreaming of the sights I was going to see and planning the photographs I was going to take." Her eyes had not lifted from the table since she started speaking. "I am ashamed now to realise how unaffected I was. My course at the Glasgow School of Art didn't start till October, but I had already met some of the other students when we went up for an Open Day during our last term at school. I had made new friends and three of us decided to go hostelling in Europe. It was the first time I had been out of the country, before the era of package holidays."

It was easier for Susan to think back to those days than to dwell on the sight that had met her at the dig site, to remember the living Elinor rather than the bones to which her body had been reduced.

"I got to know Tom then too. We could see him from the tennis court, as he helped his father hire out rowing and motor boats by the hour. His flaming red hair made him easy to pick out, even among crowds. The jetty was nearly opposite the tennis courts and was really busy. There was a steady queue of families at the busiest time and mostly Tom was there, helping them into rowing boats or motor boats, while his father looked after those who wanted to hire deck chairs for the beach."

"So he's always been involved with boats on the island?" Alice was delighted at this turn of the conversation. It would help her investigation to get some more background information about this man.

"No, he's travelled the world." Susan was used to people assuming that the islanders were lifelong stay-at-homes. "After school he studied navigation and engineering at the James Watt College in Greenock and the Glasgow College of Nautical Studies and then joined the Merchant Navy as an officer."

Alice delved deeper into her ice-cream, seeking out blueberries and raspberries in turn. Susan seemed very well informed, she thought. "Was he your boyfriend?"

"Not really. I was at the School of Art and, when he had exams for his Master's Ticket, he would study at the Mitchell

Library, the big reference library in Glasgow. We met there by chance one day and after that we saw one another if he happened to be on leave. We went to a few parties together, but then we lost touch with one another. Once he was fully qualified and travelling the world he wasn't one for letter writing. When I moved here permanently it was quite a surprise to find he was back too.

"Were you both on the island when Elinor vanished?" Alice tried to ask the question casually, but Susan was too occupied with her memories to be guarded in her response.

"Yes, but we were so concerned with our future plans that we hadn't been making much time for her. My term started in October and I was already photographing everything and anything to make up an impressive portfolio, the motion of bicycle wheels, shells, shadows, boats." Her voice tapered off, as she remembered the self-absorption that had left her no time for her friend.

"And Tom?" Alice prompted.

"Oh, Tom was spending all his time on boat maintenance. He was feeling rather guilty that he was leaving his father in the lurch, abandoning him to run the business single-handed. His father had never encouraged Tom in his ambition to become properly qualified; he felt that what had been good enough for him should satisfy his son. He had inherited a successful business from *his* father, which he had run without any book learning and he thought Tom should be satisfied to carry on the tradition."

As they sat at Susan's favourite seat, beside the window, they had been spotted and joined by Connor and Matthias who had been strolling along towards the old pier during their afternoon break. All three listened as Susan continued her story. "My parents weren't at all adventurous. Cumbrae did them fine, an ideal place to relax; my father played at the bowling green, while my mother sat and knitted lacy jumpers." She looked up at them suddenly. "I was so excited at the idea of visiting Italy and so absorbed in my own life that when I eventually did hear the news I bought into the theory that she had fled the island for a more interesting life elsewhere."

"I must be getting back." Alice rose, suddenly aware of the time they had spent on what was meant to be a short lunch break, but before she went to the counter to pay she paused a moment.

"We'll be in *The Crocodile Rock* tonight around eight. If you would like to come and meet the others that would be great."

"Thank you." Susan did not relish the idea of an evening at home and the youthful company of Alice and her friends would help her cope.

When Alice rose, Susan opted to go along at least part of the way towards the Garrison to take the long-suffering Montmorency on a quick walk, leaving Connor and Matthias to finish their coffees.

"What do you think of that story?" Connor asked trying to keep his voice neutral. When Matthias did not reply, he expanded the question. "I know she has become Alice's friend and she has a cute dog, but is it really credible that someone she had known for years disappeared mysteriously and it made so little impression on her?" Matthias frowned thoughtfully. "If we assume that she had the opportunity, what about motive and," he hesitated, seeking the right word, "and the capability. Could she have killed Elinor and buried the body in the grave where Dean found her?"

"We don't know whether Elinor was petite, but Mrs Clearsmith is a tall woman, still in good shape, even at her age. She might well have been able to drag the body to the spot, or she could have had a helper."

"I suppose the obvious accomplice would be Tom Forrest." Connor surmised. "That would tie in with the idea that Elinor was jealous of the other two. Maybe an argument developed and it got physical. Perhaps it wasn't murder. There was no plan to kill her, but once she was dead, however it happened, they panicked, buried her and scarpered as fast as they could." He saw Matthias frown slightly at the unfamiliar word. "Eh, scarper. It means to run away."

Matthias grinned as he got to his feet. "Time to get back to the museum. We have a possible scenario, but Alice won't like it," he added. "You can be the one who tells her. I would be too scared."

Alice settled back into her seat at the Museum of the Cumbraes as Professor Hughes produced some handouts of both Scottish and Norwegian records to illustrate the historical accounts of the Battle of Largs, as the background for a general discussion. "Sources on the actual battle are flimsy. The Norse version says very little, perhaps not surprisingly, because by any measurement the expedition could not be rated a success. Even if you have a primary source you have to beware. King Magnus, who commissioned his father's biography more or less immediately on his death, wanted an account that paid what he regarded as fitting tribute to his father's achievements."

"Which side lost the most men?" Connor's question was an obvious one.

"Who knows? There's plenty of information about the fleet, the names and even the nicknames of its commanders, original numbers, route and so on but there is no contemporary account of how many perished in the actual battle, so numbers vary widely in later histories."

"But the Norse account does acknowledge that the Scots won." Alice was the only one of the group who had actually read the English translation of the thirteenth century text. "The Norse sagas, in fact, claim the Scots used magic to achieve the victory."

"Maybe an ancestor of Mrs Macbeth cooked up the storm." Markus muttered to Dean.

"The entry in the Scottish chronicles written at Melrose Abbey less than a hundred years later might be expected to give a triumphant account of a Scottish victory." Alice was in full spate as she marshalled her arguments. "But these were written by monks, so the main credit for the Norse retreat is given to God. There is nothing about King Alexander's leadership, just a few words of praise for the part played by the Scottish foot soldiers."

"It seems incredible that the Norse have left absolutely no trace on the island, if they were camped here and using it as their command base." Dean wanted desperately to believe that their dig would reveal more than the bones that were seared into his memory.

"The records say that after the battle they removed their dead to a church and there is a reference to burials on the island of Bute, which would have been more firmly under Norse control at that time. The Norsemen are said to have camped at Torward Point on Cumbrae, which would have given them a good view of Largs where the Scots were waiting, but that area hasn't been examined archeologically, as yet."

DUNDONALD 1263

"Where do you think they will strike next?" King Alexander looked at his two commanders, the brothers Alexander and Walter Stewart. In the main it was a council of young men. King of Scots since the age of seven, Alexander was now twenty-two and had only taken control of his unruly kingdom last year.

Dundonald Castle, home to Alexander Stewart, High Steward of Scotland, was not large enough to accommodate a full council meeting, such as would have been held in Dunfermline Abbey, if the invasion threat had been to the eastern coast of Scotland. This was an impromptu meeting, as Alexander tried to strengthen the line of west coast fortresses against Norse landings. At the moment it was bustling with armed men, part of the force raised to combat the Norse threat. It was an ideal vantage point, commanding a view over the Mull of Kintyre, which the Norse fleet would round if they intended to threaten the mainland. The mountainous island of Arran stood out clearly on the skyline, only fifteen miles from the Scottish coast. Overland, ten miles, to the north, the Benedictine abbey of Kilwinning and the port of Irvine were danger points for a landing of the Norwegian force.

Alexander, a battle hardened crusader, had seen his brother, John, fall in Dalmetta, on the ill-fated seventh crusade, led by the pious Louis IX of France. Ironically, if Haakon had accepted Louis' invitation to join the crusade, he and Alexander could have been comrades in arms, but Haakon had refused. Now Alexander found fighting in Scotland far more to his taste than on that fated crusade. The disgraceful conflict between the Knights Templar and the Hospitallers on that crusade had made him cynical, the motivations of the crusaders tarnished. His present Scottish troops were well-armed and well-trained. Many of them were well mounted. And they were fighting in a cause he considered worthy, the defence of his realm, their homeland, from invasion.

Alexander gestured to a young page, who approached swiftly and filled their goblets.

"A bit surly that one," the king remarked.

"He'll settle," Walter grunted. "A hostage till his father pays his fines. Eighty cows he owes you, a tribute that will show us where his loyalty lies."

"MacGillivray's son?" the king's attention was caught. He looked with keener interest at the dark-haired lad, a youth of about twelve years old. "I know all about being a pawn of adults in their combats."

It was an uncomfortable topic for a king surrounded by nobles who had vied with each other for control of his person and his power through the twelve years of his minority. King at seven, married at twelve, Alexander had scores to settle when he came of age, but whilst he ruthlessly dismissed some of those who had held high offices and filled their places with his appointees, he was also pragmatic. In their own territories the two main contenders for power during his minority, Alan Durward and Walter Comyn, held sway over the people. If he wanted to raise an army, he could not afford to alienate powerful chiefs. As always he must proceed with caution, but his resentment lay deep. He looked again at the young page with some sympathy.

A father at last Alexander could even find some sympathy for MacGillivray, a farmer on the Isle of Cumbrae, even though he had still not paid his fine. God knows eighty cows fattened on the pastures of Cumbrae would be a boon to provisioning an army that already numbered thousands. But to have your child placed in danger - as a hostage – Alexander thought of his own young daughter, safe over in Dunfermline with her mother, within easy reach of the strong castles of Stirling and Edinburgh, if the invasion had come in the east. Now two years old she was an affectionate child, always able to raise a smile from her father, gurgling delightedly when he tossed her up, caught her and tossed her up again. Her birth had wakened in Alexander protective feelings that startled him; he had sired a new creature that he must now love and protect. He remembered how incensed he had been when Edward Plantagenet, his brother-in-law, had commiserated with him that the child had not been a son. He accepted that it was his duty to provide the kingdom with a male heir, but with her first glance at him, his firstborn, named Margaret after her mother, had secured a special place in his heart. His wife Margaret was pregnant again and this time might provide him with a son. Alexander prayed if he did have a son the lad would not be orphaned at seven. Knowing he could soon be fighting in battle against Haakon, he brought his attention back to the immediate danger, aware that Walter was speaking, giving an assessment of the mainland places likely to need defence.

"Magnus Olafson, so-called King of Man, has thrown in his lot with Haakon. He's attacked the mainland a few times on his way to join Haakon's fleet, some landing raids, a few farms burned but nothing major. He obviously has not learned his lesson from the last time we sent our ships against him."

Walter Stewart, Earl of Menteith and Sheriff of Ayr, had a vested interest in repelling the invaders. He held lands in Kintyre and Knapdale which were already under threat from Haakon's force. He had followed Haakon's progress down the west coast with mounting alarm. Alexander had some ships, which he had used skilfully to protect the south west mainland from falling under the influence of Magnus Olafson, King of the Isle of Man. But he had nowhere near enough sea power to match Haakon's fleet, nor were the Scots used to fighting at sea, whereas only five years previously Haakon had defeated the Danes at sea and last year had brought Iceland and Greenland under his rule.

"Haakon knows we will not fight him at sea." Alexander smiled briefly at his host's wife Jean, who had accompanied the servants into the hall and was overseeing the serving of a nourishing stew, a worried frown on her normally sonsy face. "He has plenty of men, but they are raiders, not used to meeting the kind of resistance we can put up."

"And if he thinks we are going to settle this with a javelin contest he's a wild dreamer." Stewart dismissed one of Haakon's latest suggestions scornfully. "Unless you want to take him up on it, Bailloch?"

His brother paid no attention either to the use of his nickname or to the Norse proposal that had been greeted with derision by the Scots. He had grown up used to being teased about his freckled complexion and had long since abandoned the habit of fighting those who tried to provoke him by calling him Freckly Face. He had, however, developed a reputation for not backing off from a fight.

This time, though, he had made sure that, like him, all the Scots under his command were fully prepared for battle and not in the slightest tempted by these odd alternative suggestions being put forward in all seriousness by Haakon's envoys.

"It does show that Haakon fears to meet us on land. Lightning raids are more to his liking – and he's damned good at it. When his ships appear on the horizon they are only an hour from landing. Time for flight if you are quick enough, but not to assemble forces for a fight. I can understand why the chiefs of the Western Isles pay homage to him and look to him to settle their disputes. One day we may be able to protect them, but that day is not yet come."

"He will have heard of our present strength." King Alexander was young, but he had a good grasp of strategy. "Thank God the English have at last paid up Margaret's dowry." He was fully aware of the advantages and drawbacks of having the king of England for a father-in-law. "Not a minute too soon. Equipping an army is no small affair. We have been married for a dozen years and had to wait all that time for the English gold. My blessed grand dame, St Margaret, is on our side too. There have been signs of her saintly intervention over at Dunfermline."

As the descendant of a saint, Alexander was carefully pious. The Stewart brothers nodded solemnly in agreement. Their experience of crusading had diminished rather than increased their *piety, but they knew the advantage to morale to have a saint on your side.*

CUMBRAE 1263

The season when the brambles were at their sweetest was no time for sea battles. Her father's ships were the best in the world and his sailors too, but against the full force of the autumn winds, headway was impossible. It was futile to try to fight. Some of his force were safely riding the storm in the more sheltered bay to the south, but powerless to help those in danger.

On the hill above, Ragnhild watched the longships struggle against the force of the sea. At this height she could not see her father below, standing on a small mound near the high tide point of the Cumbrae coast, fuming at his impotence against the weather. She did not know then that he had been ashore on the Scottish mainland with his men, but had been persuaded to retire to Cumbrae to organise reinforcements for the Norsemen, who were faring badly against the Scots.

Ironically it was a point he had made much of in 'The King's Mirror.' He had ignored the wisdom acquired in a lifetime at the helm of a seafaring nation, advice he was accustomed to give to young men still learning the craft of seamanship. After October, he had warned, the sea begins to be very restless and the tempests increase in violence, blowing the waves into a froth; the south wind is no longer a friend and brings a mantle of grey clouds and heavy rain. Huge billows, chilling scud and wide-breasted waves seem to seek out ships to destroy them. All sensible men, he had observed, set sail while summer is at its best; for then one is not likely to meet misfortune. Now, through his own obstinate contriving, he was in danger of losing all the profit which he had gained in his summer campaign.

Ragnhild had the same view right across the firth as

Haakon had from his vantage point, but from higher up. She had chosen a spot where the track was open to the east but lined by a higher, bracken-topped bank which provided some limited cover from wind and rain. Physically she was warm, and comparatively dry, her fur-lined cloak and hood were of the best, but her mind was with the human creatures being claimed by the sea, as boats were overwhelmed by the high waves.

Their lives were lost in trying to prevent the treasure ship from following the few boats that had foundered already on the coast opposite, where the Scottish force was drawn up. The anchors of the treasure ship could not hold against the tides. The ferocious wind and the currents were dragging it nearer and nearer the dangerous coast. Other ships were sent with much needed manpower to help the crew bring the ship under control. As they attempted to board, sailors dropped into the sea; the forces of nature proved too powerful for human strength.

Harald was with the fleet.

Despite her warm cloak, she shivered. Although she had desperately wanted to keep him safe, Ragnhild had not tried to dissuade him.

"I am Haakon's man," he declared. He had been miserably unhappy, torn between what he knew to be his duty to her and his sense of honour. "I pledged myself to fight for him. If I break that bond in an hour of danger, I would live a dishonoured coward."

Despite herself, Ragnhild knew if she had been able to marry Harald in Norway she would have joined the many women whose men faced perils on sea and land. All she could do now was what wives, mothers and daughters had done in the past and would do in the future, pray for the safe return of their menfolk.

Harald came back.

He had been one of those who had accomplished the rescue of the treasure ship, taking over the steering oar from the exhausted helmsman and holding on grimly, with the help of others who scrambled aboard and joined in the fight to control the bucking vessel. All their practice in archery and martial exercises, as well as regular rowing, gave them the upper body strength to haul on the rain-soaked canvas and fight the wind. At first all they could do was prevent the ship from running aground to become a windfall for the Scots. Gradually however they were able to angle the sails to catch the rare sporadic gusts that helped them steer the ship out of danger and round the tip of the island into the comparative safety of a western bay, where the water, though choppy, was not like the churning maelstrom of the last hour.

◆ ◆ ◆

Before Bjornvig departed with the fleet, Harald visited the camp for a last time. Ragnhild remained near their new home, perched high above, where she could at least see the ships as they assembled for departure. In the camp, the stories were already firming into legend.

Ogmund Krækidants, the Crowdancer, was celebrated as a hero.

"You should have seen how he fought!" a youngish warrior said with awed admiration. "I'd heard of berserkers, but now I know what it looks like to see one in action. He was everywhere, taking on one Scot after another."

"They attacked us when we were setting up a shield wall, so that the ships that had been grounded by the storm could get afloat again," a brawny warrior, whom Harald did not know grunted. "Then those nidderings cast off without us." The widespread anger at this mistake still rankled.

"How many fought? How many were slain?" Sigvat Bodvarson was one of the Icelandic contingent who had joined Haakon's fleet. Well born, of an influential family, he had been one of the muster role for Haakon's flagship on the journey through the Hebrides, but like many he had been on Arran when the storm had scattered the fleet. The storm had abated, the force of the gale spent, and other ships and men had now arrived on the scene, battle ready and eager for news. The large group round the campfire contained both newly arrived warriors and combatants in the latest battle. Sigvat led the questioning.

Ivar Helgason shrugged. "Nine hundred?" There was a question in his voice. "Five longships and the transport ship at the start."

"It was magic." Arni Stinkar was one of those who wore an amulet with Thor's hammer under his tunic, but there were plenty of nods and mutters of agreement from the assembled warriors.

"Aye the Scots had powerful magicians who brewed up the storm." He indicated the now calm waters where the longships rose and fell gently on the ebbing tide.

Sigvat ignored him. "How many slain?" he repeated.

"Not many at first. Wounds rather than death blows. The Scots rained missiles on us that stung but did not kill. The lashing rain and wind were our allies then. It was hard for their archers to find their targets."

"But easier for their slingshot." Ivar rubbed his shoulder ruefully. His bruises had darkened and still pained him, but his skin was unbroken. "Our shield wall held, though we were outnumbered. Few Scots fell. They kept their distance, content to rely on javelins, sling shot and arrows,"

Sigvat knew his uncle would expect a full account of his adventures and the fate of the fleet, if God granted him a safe homecoming. Then his report would provide the strong framework like the warp yarns on the loom through which his uncle would weave a saga with the strands of poetry. Later Sigvat's uncle, Sturla Thordarson, one of the most famous bards in the north, would weave the tale into a shape that could be sung in halls for centuries, his nephew's eye witness account underpinning the poetry.

"There was little we could do to help the forces who were fighting on the Scottish strand. We were fighting the worst storm I have ever known. Masts had to be thrown down. No anchors were holding. We did not control our direction. The tempest decided where we went. It was the next day before reinforcements could be sent."

"I hear Haakon took to a long ship." The Icelander had mixed feelings about the monarch, whose last war had been to subdue Iceland and bring it under Norwegian rule. His seamanship,

leadership and courage, however, drew his unstinting admiration.

Later, the friends sat on the shore with a large rock behind them that rose up like a lion. Harald wondered if a Scottish bard would weave it into a saga for the Scots king, Alexander, whose lion banner had defeated Haakon's ravens.

"It is over," Bjornvig said. "The Western Isles and Orkney will stay within Norway's area of influence, but they say the Scottish king has sworn that Cumbrae, Bute and Arran will always be part of his realm. That means that here you will both be safe."

It was no surprise when, before his departure, Haakon ordered much of the cargo of the treasure ship to be unloaded. The dangers of trusting such a vast amount to the hold of one ship had been all too clearly demonstrated in the last few hours. It was also one of the most suitable ships to hold the bodies of those slain in the battle for future burial. Ragnhild had heard that, in pagan times, her ancestors placed their chiefs in boats when they died and set the boats on fire, Now the burning boats that she could see across on the Scottish mainland had been set alight on Haakon's orders to prevent them falling into Scottish hands. Nor was it surprising that the Norsemen, sent by Haakon to destroy the boats, were able to land unchallenged on the former battlefield. They were still a formidable force. The Scots seemed content with what success they had already achieved and, satisfied that the danger of another attack had passed, had retired to let the Norse collect their dead.

Never had Haakon felt the forty-six years of his reign weigh more heavily on his shoulders. He had led his men into battle, but he had not stayed out the fight. He had allowed himself to be taken out of danger, persuaded to board a barge bound for Cumbrae and stand impotently on the other side of the water, while his men fought both human and elemental enemies. He bitterly regretted that he had remained alive to give the order to set sail for home, but it was one of the duties of a king to save what he could: men, ships and reputation.

Now that the ship was safe, some of the treasure would be entered into the exchequer rolls as the expenses of building and fitting out ships now wrecked on the Scottish coast. Some would pay his men and his allies. Some would be set aside for future negotiations with the King of Scots, in case he was prepared to relinquish his claim to sovereignty of the isles in return for payment.

Unloading the ship was one of the last duties Harald accomplished as one of Haakon's men. Although the west of the island was more sheltered, the men still had the weather to contend with. The chaos of the repulse was still in evidence, as men struggled ashore with chests and leather bags and deposited them on the beach above the high tide mark. Some were immediately earmarked for transfer to Haakon's ship. Others were put aside for later decision, all this in the face of strong winds and steady downpours. Norsemen worked alongside men from the Western Isles and the Isle of Man. When the seashore was clear again, there was no certainty that everything was accounted for and that none of it had found its way into other pockets.

As he worked, Harald could see that Rudri, the conqueror of Bute, had chosen a spot further inshore, despite the extra work involved in carrying the burdens the additional distance. Rudri's reputation was in tatters after his dishonourable behaviour during the recent attack on the castle of Bute. There the garrison had been forced to surrender and had been promised that they would be allowed to leave safely, a promise that had been broken. These deaths ensured his ignominy even among men who admired ruthlessness. But Haakon was a pragmatist. Rudri was fighting for him, because Alexander had refused to confirm his right to rule the island of Bute. Haakon contested Alexander's right to overlordship and was prepared to allocate Bute to Rudri in return for his fealty, fully aware that Rudri's only loyalty was to himself and his own advancement.

Rudri was untrustworthy, but he also possessed guile. Visibility was poor, so only a couple of henchmen, the brothers Ewan and Angus, knew of his nefarious activities. In the disorder it was simple for him to conceal a substantial hoard that could be collected later in an easy voyage across from Bute to Cumbrae. When the main cargo had been reloaded, this time onto three ships, the *toilers retired to seek shelter for the night, get dry and fed, and warm their insides with liquor.*

It was an easy matter to lag behind the others as they strode out rapidly back to camp. Rudri had already chosen a place for his cache. He knew the territory, this part of the island immediately opposite the castle he now possessed on Bute. The rocky cliff face did not have any caves, but there were fissures. In one that he had explored in more peaceful times there was a ledge jutting out but angled towards the sky, so that there was a wedge-shaped hiding place just above head height for a tall man like Rudri. He had only ever used it to store fishing gear and a hunting bow, but now it offered an ideal place of concealment. Raised on the cupped hand of Ewan, he took the bags from Angus and packed them carefully along the shelf, before dropping back to the ground. A blend of bribery and threats should keep his helpers silent, long enough at least till he could ensure their permanent silence. Together they set off back to the camp, where Rudri increased his profit, when Haakon began the process of distributing rewards to those of his allies who were departing for their own lands. Grimly he earmarked a small bag of silver coins for the mother of Ewan and Angus, who would soon be mourning her sons.

The next day was a perfect example of the fickle autumn weather. The grey clouds of the morning were replaced by bright sunshine. Tiny white clouds speckled the blue sky, with only a band of dark grey nearer the horizon. The grass and the bracken were as motionless as a ship becalmed. Towards the evening the clouds were tinged with gold.

One by one the ships departed to the northwest; only Magnus of Man sailed south, already regretting that he had chosen the wrong side and fearing Alexander's reprisals once he no longer had the protection of Haakon's fleet. Rudri had to take ship without his haul, but that had always been likely. With feigned piety he accompanied the body of Andrew Holm, one of Haakon's most trusted captains, whom Haakon had decided was to be buried on Bute. It was a task he could not escape; Haakon had given him five warships to help him subdue Bute. He was sure his secret would be safe until he could return to fetch it.

His plan, though, would "gang agley."

The folk of Bute did not need to have long memories to have reason to hate him. There were nine families grieving for the men of the garrison he had slaughtered, and others lamenting deaths and loss when he burnt and butchered mercilessly. Vengeance stalked him.

Weeks, months, years, decades, centuries passed. No-one penetrated the narrow fissure; the hoard lay undisturbed, nestled safely out of sight.

CUMBRAE 2005

Alice's indulgence at lunchtime had left her with little appetite and she toyed with Mrs Macbeth's offering that evening.

"I don't believe it." Alice shook her head vigorously, sending her red-gold curls flying from side to side. "I haven't known Susan very long, but long enough to know she isn't capable of this."

As Matthias had foretold, Alice had reacted indignantly to the case they had constructed against Susan Clearsmith.

"Still," Paul remarked, "Crime Scene Photographer? Taking pictures of dead bodies is odd work for a woman. I mean a person," he amended as Alice turned her blazing blue eyes on him. He had not meant to be provocative, an unusual occurrence, he realised, in a rare moment of self-awareness.

"I suppose the bottom line is that we don't know enough about the kind of person Elinor was, or the circumstances that led to her death." Dean's intervention took the spotlight off the squabble. "We don't even know if the police are treating this as murder, or what they found at the site."

"And we are unlikely to find out. I can't see the police taking us into their confidence, but maybe the people they have interviewed would give us some information about the questions they are asking." Kathryn's contributions to the conversation were rare, but in the end her suggestions were agreed, as the next steps in their search for the truth of Elinor's death.

When Susan arrived at *The Crocodile Rock* that evening, Alice moved along the bench to make room for her. She and the others were seated at two booths near the frosted window that had an engraving of a head of crocodile protruding from a stylised sea. Swiftly she introduced Susan to the rest.

"We are an international lot," she explained. Kathryn is from Swansea, Markus from Heidelberg, Paul is English, although he is studying at St Andrews. Dean, who is over at the bar, is our token Scot. The others are in the booth next door. Both Markus and Paul had risen to greet Susan, a courtesy that was going out of fashion, she thought. Paul remained standing.

"Can I get you a drink?" he asked and made his way over to the bar to get her a glass of white wine, passing Dean on his way back with their order.

"I met Mrs Clearsmith when I fell in love with her dog at the West Bay park." Alice and Susan were now on first name terms, but, given the age gap, the formality seemed more fitting. She was at Glasgow School of Art."

"Many decades ago." Susan smiled. I majored, as the Americans would say, in photography."

"It must be hard, though to make a living at that." Kathryn was genuinely interested. "If you take photographs of a child and the parents don't like it, you've nothing to show for all the time, effort and materials you've expended.

"Can you tell Kathryn is studying accountancy?" Dean smiled at her. "We're hoping she'll advise us how to make a fortune when we eventually start earning."

"It will cost you," teased Kathryn. "No discounts even for friends."

"So you aren't all studying archaeology?"

"No, the aim is that the group is multidisciplinary as well as international. Markus here is a medic. There are two others that aren't here."

As Dr O'Flaherty passed the table he looked curiously at the stranger in their midst. Paul caught the glance and decided an introduction was in order.

"Mrs Clearsmith, this is one of our tutors, Dr O'Flaherty. Sir, Mrs Clearsmith lives in Millport. We have been telling her about the archaeological project." Paul included the *sir* from his usual sense of devilment, but O'Flaherty's response was genial.

"If you squeeze up, I'll join you for a bit, long enough anyway to miss my turn to buy a round over there." He never missed a chance to foster good relations with the local populace. "Have you always lived on Cumbrae, Mrs Clearsmith?"

When Susan had replied with a brief outline of her early visits, and how the attractions of the island had led her to settle there, O'Flaherty nodded with understanding.

"Ah, yes. It's a return for me too. I once took part in a dig when I was a young student. Professor Hughes was there too. We even congregated in this very pub to play and sing folk music."

"I remember that," Susan exclaimed.

She was not surprised that there was no flicker of recognition from O'Flaherty as he acknowledged her comment. It would have been astonishing if he had seen, in this older woman with the smartly-cropped grey hair, the young teenager with a dark brown mane fashionably obscuring one side of her face. She had sat timidly in the corner seat, mesmerised by the students. Their confidence and vitality attracted her and she wondered if Art School would transform her into one of these exotic creatures. Susan even recalled the young O'Flaherty. Her trained artist's eyes saw behind the now thickened body to the rather stocky broad shouldered young man he had once been. Folk songs were in fashion and he had been one of the leaders of the singing, glass in one hand, pipe in the other. That Hughes had been there too, she could well believe, but he had not secured a place in her memory.

"You were on the island when Elinor vanished," she remarked.

"We were with the archaeological dig yes," said Hughes,

"but we had gone by the time she disappeared." When the police officer told us which day she went missing, I was able to check back the research notes I made at that time for my Masters degree. I had looked up the old file for reference when planning this current project, so it was on my laptop. We left the day before her disappearance. Both of us, and quite a few of the others, travelled up to Glasgow together, where we split up.

"Then I had a three-hour journey to catch the ferry to Belfast and I hitched from there back to Dublin. No cheap airlines in those days for poor students." O'Flaherty chipped in.

Alice and the others noted the alibi, but Susan remained lost in her own memories of the summer Elinor disappeared. At seventeen Elinor could not go into the pub, She and Tom, a few months older, could attend the impromptu folk singing in the bar lounge. She remembered how grown-up she had felt, sitting with her Babycham, tapping her feet to the beat of Scots, Irish and American folk songs.

Sitting beside O'Flaherty, she was suddenly aware of another memory. Now that smoking was banned in pubs you became more keenly aware of the smell of smoke and she recollected that particular odour.

"Is it possible I remember you too? Did you smoke a pipe in those days?"

"Then and now." He patted his pocket. "Pipe tobacco was not the substance of choice for young people then and I always liked to be a bit different. It started as an affectation, but it became an addiction." He rose, nodding briefly to them. "I see the danger of buying the next round is past," he joked, and headed to the table he shared with Alan.

When Tom entered the bar he was surprised to see Susan ensconced in a booth with a crowd of young people. Most of them were strangers to him, but he did a double take when he saw Dean, whom he had last seen peddling desperately towards Millport, without a word of explanation or indeed thanks for extricating him from a collapsed tent. He now knew that this must be the lad who had discovered the body.

There was room for six people in the booth so when she saw Tom looking in their direction Susan quickly asked if he might join them before beckoning him over.

"We've met before, though there was no time for a formal introduction." Tom held out his hand and smiled at Dean.

"I'm Tom Forrest."

After one glance at Dean, Tom decided not to raise the topic of the circumstances of their last meeting. Beneath the lad's healthy outdoor complexion, he was pale and his mouth had narrowed into an expression of distress.

Alice too had noticed Dean's reaction and took the conversation back to the issue of smoking.

"I, for one, am glad that smoking isn't allowed in pubs any more. I can't even stand running the gauntlet of passing the smokers who stand at the door of pubs to get their nicotine fix." She wrinkled her nose in disgust, remembering the aroma of tobacco smoke that clung to O'Flaherty's jacket on the peg at the hostel. "Hardly any of us smoke," she said looking round, noticing that Paul had the good grace to look slightly ashamed.

"I smoked a pipe myself for many years," Tom confessed. I probably took it up because it seemed to go with the naval image. "I stopped years ago, but I must say that once it becomes a habit, you are never quite rid of it. At the end of a meal I still feel the urge to light up." He avoided any temptation to warn them not to start smoking; young people made up their own minds and would be unlikely to listen to superfluous advice.

Alice woke once again to clear blue skies. The sunlight and the smell of the sea drew her outside and she turned northwards to walk a little upriver in the direction of the dig site and Haakon's mound. It was surprising, she mused, how the group dynamics had settled: she was happy to pair off with Dean; Kathryn and Paul also seemed to be forging a friendship; Matthias, with a steady girlfriend back home, was friendly with all;

Graziella too was content to be friends with everyone and often she, Connor and Markus formed a trio, fostered by their common interest in music.

A cormorant sat watchfully on a rock, while its mate plunged spectacularly into the sea. Oystercatchers waded across the patches of sand, digging their graceful slender beaks under the surface, the creatures of the natural world in their constant search for sustenance. She turned back towards the hostel and breakfast.

"We decided to work here in the hostel, as we've heard from the police that by the end of today the site will be released for us to continue the dig." Alan Hughes examined the group in front of him for any sign of reluctance, but saw only solemn looks of acceptance. "We're also considering opening a small dig a few hundred yards further north on the coastal side of the road, a site where one old map mentions a possible burial site. That would show you on a smaller scale how a new site is assessed and a dig started.

"Meanwhile we have something different for you. A local gentleman has a significant collection of Viking weapons, authentic and replicas. He has kindly agreed to bring along a selection of these and give a brief talk after the coffee break.

Sandy Gordon appeared punctually, bearing a long bag of coarse canvas from which he proudly produced his shield, seax and asgautr and laid them out lovingly on a cloth which he had spread on the table.

"The fingertip search is completed," Andrew reported, when DI Evans appeared for their morning meeting. "Everything is bagged, but the list of items is not promising. There's absolutely nothing that we could ascribe to the time the body was buried. Of course it doesn't help that the site has been used by so many people during the dig. Any find will have to be cross checked to eliminate the possibility that it's theirs. That said there's little to check." He handed Evans the print-out despondently.

"Perhaps this will cheer you up a bit." Evans glanced briefly at Andrew's list and then slid it aside. "This is our first real clue. Full details will be faxed over, but some shreds of pipe tobacco were attached to the remaining fragments of clothing. I think we can be reasonably sure that our seventeen-year-old female victim didn't smoke a pipe, but she certainly came into contact with someone who did, perhaps a work colleague, a customer, a friend, a killer."

After Andrew had written the information on the white incident board, he added the words *What kind? Whose? When?* "It would be asking too much that a rare type of tobacco, only sold in a few outlets in the United Kingdom by salesmen who know most of their customers personally."

Evans smiled indulgently. "If you have any thoughts of applying to the CID, wean yourself off Sherlock Holmes stories. Most of police work is footslogging, getting witnesses, piecing together the evidence. But you might start asking if any of the suspects were pipe smokers. You do the house to house, and collar any local you meet on the street as well. I thought I'd have a look at where she lived, though I doubt if there would be any fingerprints or other clues there, unless that was where she got her fatal injury and traces of her blood have survived."

In less than ten minutes Evans was climbing the outside staircase leading to the small flat where Elinor and her mother had lived. It was on the first floor of a two storey building, half way up the broad street that led up from the old harbour. Although there was an entry door on the street, it was locked. Three names were inserted into plastic nameplates beside a buzzer and when Evans pressed on the first he was answered by a young woman, who agreed readily to his request for some moments of her time, suggesting that he come through to the back and up the external staircase to her door.

A first glance at the flat told him that the mission was fruitless. No features of a 1970s flat remained. The laminated wooden floors were brightened with rugs. The kitchen featured integrated units and marble worktops and the bathroom had become a wet room with smooth grey and silver laminated walls and modern porcelain fittings.

Nor could the owner add anything to his investigation. She and her husband had owned the flat for only a few years, using it as a holiday home in the time honoured way traditional on the island, a perfect bolt-hole from the city, close to a beach where their toddler could paddle and make sand pies. They had bought the flat through the local estate agent and the sellers had also been using it as a holiday home. Andrew made a note to check out the estate agent's records, if they existed, but it was far down his priority list. He felt he could draw a fairly firm line under this particular line of enquiry.

Meanwhile, armed with some specific questions, Andrew had set off along the row of shops and houses that fringed the bay.

"What do you remember about the time Elinor Sommers vanished?"

He found this a useful way to approach folk, although he had to be patient when trivia that could never be relevant to the enquiry were described in tedious detail. Someone's grand-children had won the sand building competition with a relief version of the Indian Rock; the Brownies had got filthy in the fancy dress competition because they had travelled in the back of the coal lorry dressed as sunflowers. Summer activities on Cumbrae had not changed much over decades, but he did learn that Elinor had entered for a Beautiful Bathing Belles competition that summer, one of a range of events that began with the Bonny Babies and ended with the Glamorous Grannies. Several people still had photographs of the event. It seemed Elinor had been one of a group of giggling girls that had dared each other to compete. For the first time Andrew was able to see the young girl as she had been within weeks of her death. The photograph was black and white but Elinor's smooth fair hair was tucked behind her ears and brought forward to hang loose over a spotted swimsuit. Her lithe shapely legs and neat waist, the result of hours on the tennis court, had not been enough to secure her the title, which had gone to a much more generously endowed summer visitor, but it was another way Elinor could have come to the attention of her killer and Andrew duly recorded it for transfer to his incident board.

The other strand of his investigation had been to find out the purchasers of pipe tobacco on the island. Several newsagents kept a stock of both cigarettes and tobacco. He quickly discovered that the large newsagents at the old pier had the greatest selection and, although the proprietor at the time was long dead, he was able to get some idea of the tobacco trade then. Sandy Gordon was his best source. Not only did he smoke a pipe now, but he had also had a Saturday job at the newsagents, having been promoted from the daily paper round he had done as a youngster.

"Back then I smoked cigarettes and a pipe," he explained. "Wherever possible other people's cigarettes," he laughed. "Actually that was one good reason for switching to the pipe. The custom then was to hand round your cigarette packet and later others would reciprocate. It was a pricey custom, even though cigarettes were far cheaper then. Pipe smoking was less costly. No-one expected you to offer them a fill of your pipe. The advertisements promoted it as a good way to attract women, the choice of men of action and sophistication, the tobacco companies must have spent a fortune on television advertisements." Sandy looked down at his knitted cardigan covering his modest paunch. "In actual fact, though, it was the old men at the bowling green who were the best customers then."

Back at the police station, after a morning of interviewing, Andrew added Sandy Gordon to the board, his only entry so far under pipe smokers. Sandy had been very helpful, but that was no guarantee of innocence. Often perpetrators liked to become involved in investigations, getting some sort of extra thrill at pretending to cooperate. He flicked through his notebook despondently. People had been keen to talk, excited at the idea of being involved, even if they were saddened at the thought of the death. He felt nearer to an understanding of the kind of person Elinor had been, her personality and background filled in. Everything that Susan Clearsmith had said had been confirmed. No one had missed Elinor till halfway through the day of her disappearance.

"Elinor never gave her mother a moment of trouble," he had been told by her primary school teacher, who at ninety was still a stalwart of the local bridge club.

"She would be called a single parent nowadays. Her husband died when Elinor was a toddler and Mrs Sommers considered herself lucky that she had a trade where she could earn her livelihood and stay at home. Elinor never came home to an empty house, but she was a self-sufficient lass, since when she did come home she found her mother beavering away all the hours that God sent."

For Andrew a clear picture emerged. At the time of Elinor's disappearance, her widowed mother had worked late into the night finishing a set of curtains for a demanding customer and, when she rose the next morning and set out to deliver and hang the curtains, she had assumed Elinor had left for work. Her skill as a seamstress and dressmaker won her a steady enough income; even some dress shops on the mainland sent their more expensive gowns to be altered. Her reputation depended on the quality of her work and the certainty of delivery.

"Do you remember anyone else who was friendly with Elinor?"

Jane Harris gave him a withering look. His question had been straightforward, but he realised his informant had taken umbrage at the idea that her memory was failing. Andrew had no difficulty believing that she could have quelled the unruliest of pupils. "If you come back later today, or tomorrow, I'll give you a list. I can tell you though that she had no best friend but also no enemies. She had a wee group of chums that stuck together, joined the Brownies, learned tap dancing, started wearing lipstick. Like Elinor most of them left school and went straight into employment in shops and other businesses in the town. Securing a coveted job with the council was quite a success for Elinor.

It was not long before the significance of pipe tobacco was generally known. Although the details of the finding of a strand in Elinor's clothing were not clear, the island grapevine was quick to notice the trend of the questions that Andrew had been asking and speculation was rife in the various venues where the gossips met. This put Fraser McCrone at *The Crocodile* Rock in an ideal position to gather all the latest breaking news and he had become the students' main informant.

"It's a disadvantage to us that we don't know what the police are finding out," Dean said, after listening to Connor's latest snippets. "We need to know why they are asking about tobacco. Do you think if we made friends with the police constable he would give us any information?"

"Seriously?" Alice rejected the suggestion firmly. "I think there is no chance. Not if he has any sense. If he goes blabbing about the process of the investigation to all and sundry, he would perhaps be alerting the perpetrator. He might be young, but he's not daft."

"In any case can we not make an educated guess?" Paul stirred his coffee thoughtfully before continuing. "Surely they must have found some tobacco at the site, but it would need to be more specific than that. They must know the doc smokes, although not on site as far as I know, but his tobacco could easily have found its way to the ground there. But the body was buried so if some was found on it, then it could easily have come from whoever buried her."

Dean nodded in acknowledgement of the logic of Paul's argument. He did not relish the memory of his gruesome discovery, but he forced himself to think of it more dispassionately. "I'm sure if there was any tobacco on the body it wouldn't have come from surface contamination. I think we have a working theory that we should try to take further.

"It does throw suspicion on the doc. He was on the spot back then, though there's nothing to connect him to Elinor."

Later, Mrs Macbeth thought, with some justification, that it was cupboard love that had prompted some of the lads to help her carry the baskets of sheets, pillowcases and duvet covers from the laundry to the linen store. The smell of her homemade shortbread filled the kitchen and adjoining corridor as she transferred some '*petticoat tails*' onto a plate.

"Why don't you take a break?" Connor said, gesturing towards the French windows which had been slid back to cool the kitchen down. Outside there was a garden table and chairs.

His charm worked and soon the group were clutching mugs of tea, munching shortbread and drawing Mrs Macbeth out on life on Cumbrae.

"I was intrigued by something the prof said about you, at our introduction. He said you like Berthold Brecht - and there were some other names I can't remember.

Mary Macbeth smiled tolerantly. "Typical of him to remember that. I've been in the Dramatic Society, since I was a teenager, long before I met my husband and acquired a name that some people still claim is bad luck to utter in a theatre. Our plays are part of the summer entertainment programme. We have one show a week, a different one the next week and then we repeat them, as most visitors just stay for two weeks. A lot depends on how strong the company is at any specific time. The *Threepenny Opera* was one of our more ambitious ventures, a winter project. We tend to keep the summer shows light, drawing room comedies, mostly murder mysteries and farces, if we have enough comic talent at the time."

"You were in the Brecht?"

"I was Pirate Jenny." Mrs Macbeth smiled nostalgically. "It was a strong part. We didn't do it again in the summer, as not everyone was available, but we did present a few scenes, as part of a musical medley programme, in *The Crocodile Rock.* That was where I first met Dr Hughes and Dr O'Flaherty, who were both in folk song groups. But I must be getting on." She rose purposefully, and started to fetch out the ingredients for the evening meal. Taking the hint, Connor rose and led the others from the kitchen.

"Pirate Jenny?" he said as they headed to the snooker room. "Is the play some kind of pantomime?"

"Hardly," said Markus drily. "It's a serious play, with songs. You'll probably know the song *Mack the Knife.* It's one of the most famous."

Connor nodded. "The penny's dropped. It was the pirate name that misled me. I do know the *Mack the Knife* song, of course, powerful stuff, though I've never seen the play. Who's this Jenny?"

"She's quite a macabre character. She's a hotel maid, resentful of how contemptuously she's treated by the people of the town. She imagines a pirate ship entering the harbour, firing on all the houses and flattening them. When the pirates allow Jenny to decide the fate of the townspeople, she orders them all killed and sails off with them."

"Help! I hope Mrs Macbeth was chosen for her acting ability, not for her similarity to the role. We haven't given her any cause to despise us, have we? Otherwise we could be in trouble."

"I suppose we all tend to take people for granted. If they are behind a till in a supermarket or serving tables at a restaurant, we don't really think of their lives or how they might be feeling."

Connor had barely listened. His thoughts had taken a new direction. "Everyone was so interconnected that summer. If Mrs Macbeth was emotionally committed to her part she might have at least compiled a list of those people she would have taken revenge on for how they had treated her in the past. Do you think Elinor would have been on that list?"

As planned, Mrs Macbeth had been told that no evening meal was needed as Graziella had arranged a carry-out meal from the Fish and Chip shop at the harbour. The evening was mild and quite suitable for eating outdoors on the benches facing the little tidal harbour, where small craft bobbed on the high tide. Most had chosen fish and Graziella, who had done her own preliminary research, explained gravely to Markus and Matthias that a fish supper meant that it was served with chips. Paul pointed out the availability of a sausage supper, in case they were feeling homesick, while Markus countered by daring Paul to try the Haggis balls and Matthias looked speculatively from him to the water and asked him if he could swim.

It was generally felt that the coincidence of both Elinor's death and the discovery of her body taking place during two archaeological digs, separated by thirty years but both attended by the same two men, could not be dismissed as just a twist of fate.

In *The Crocodile Rock*, Alice eyed the two men curiously. "To think we have two potential suspects in front of us. Don't you think it's too much of a coincidence that both of them were on the island just before Elinor disappeared?"

"Coincidence is always suspicious in fiction at least," Dean agreed, but even if the timing is right we'd need a motive."

"A young attractive girl? She might have rejected an advance, or on the other hand been spurned by the handsome talented young man she had been pestering."

Dean raised an eyebrow quizzically, noting in passing that the practice was yielding results. He was less successful in assessing O'Flaherty's potential sex appeal to a nubile teenager. It strained credulity, he decided. O'Flaherty had not aged particularly well, the signs of his lifestyle choices evident in his complexion and build. Could he possibly have been attractive thirty years ago?

Alice caught his incredulous look.

"He's funny. He can make people laugh. Magazine articles

always say a good sense of humour is vital. He's a popular lecturer, good entertainment, but not so popular in tutorials. I've never had him, but the word is that he's quite lazy about turning up on time, returning essays and so on. He's presented quite a few television programmes and is maybe more interested in that than teaching students."

◆ ◆ ◆

"Now that we have Alexander Gordon on the list of potential suspects we need far more information about his background and his relationship with Elinor. How long has he lived in Cumbrae? How well did he know Elinor? What was he doing on the day she disappeared? At present we are assuming that was when she died. I'll take over that part." Dai Evans outranked him, but Andrew was not reluctant to turn this witness over to him.

"It's not exactly a good cop, bad cop routine," Evans continued, "but, if this line of enquiry comes to nothing, I can shoulder any resentment he might feel better than you can, as the police officer serving this community. What do you know about him?"

"He was an accountant. When I came here he was already retired, but he's involved in quite a lot of island activities, often as the treasurer. He also audits the accounts for voluntary activities, without as far as I know charging for his work. I've always regarded him as a local, but whether he was born and raised here I don't know."

"Easily found out." Evans closed his notebook after getting Gordon's address and strode purposely from the station. It took him less than fifteen minutes to reach Gordon's house. The interview began well. Evans knew the value of flattery in lulling a suspect into a false sense of security.

"My colleague has told me how helpful you have been and what a mine of information you are. How long have you lived in Millport?"

Alexander Gordon responded like a dog to his handler's whistle. "All my life," he answered. "My father was a town councillor and was almost elected provost." Even decades later the failure of the Millport residents to award his father this honour still rankled. "I followed him into his accountancy business, and inherited the company on his death."

Evans had written fewer than ten words in his notebook.

"Quite a small place this. Was there really enough work for two people?"

"You obviously don't know how accountancy works. Plenty of people needed their books done for the taxman and my father had a substantial number of clients on the mainland."

Evans found the man's smugness, pomposity and air of superiority irritating, but none of these defects were crimes.

"It's vital for us to get a sense of what Elinor Sommers was like, as I'm sure you know only too well. What kind of background detail can you give us that would help us compile as full a picture as possible?"

The man puffed out his chest proudly as he started his narrative.

Evans subdued a sigh. He had after all brought the deluge of detail on himself and could only hope that the outcome was worthwhile.

When he learned they had gone through primary school in the same class, he interrupted to speed up the narrative.

"How did you get on with Elinor when you were a teenager? Were you and she in the same group of friends?"

Sandy shook his head. I wasn't in her league. Elinor and the other girls weren't interested in a skinny, spotty, bespectacled teenager whose only accomplishment was to be top of the class in maths and arithmetic." Evans drew a double line under the name in his notebook. The man seemed to be disarmingly honest, but the strength of teenage resentment was not to be discounted. If he had made amorous overtures and had been rebuffed, he might have lashed out in anger.

"What about clubs and leisure activities? I know Elinor

played tennis."

"There were public courts in the grounds of the Garrison that people just booked. I didn't play. But now that I come to think of it," His face showed the dawning of a new memory, "the Dramatic Society was always in search of people for bit parts, especially young people. Elinor's mother made most of the costumes and I'm sure Elinor was roped in for bit parts, as I was, but we were never in the same show. I discovered I liked acting but I moved on to historical re-enactments. Locally, the main event is over in Largs, where there is a Viking Festival. I've been a mediaeval Norseman and a Scot, the costume and weaponry are more or less the same."

"Weaponry?"

"My shield, seax and asgautr are mounted above my fireplace, "Sandy boasted proudly. "Nowadays I tend to use a foam sword for events."

Evans knew that forensics had found evidence of rock particles to account for the death. Could a hefty sword-hilt inflict similar damage? He drew a third line under the other two.

◆ ◆ ◆

When Evans returned to the police station he found Andrew leafing through a pile of papers spread out around a manila folder that lay beside him on the table. This has just arrived from the police archives. It has the basic records of the initial 1972 investigation, the mother's missing person report and her statement, and statements of all the others who were interviewed."

"Anything interesting?"

"A few things. When Mrs Clearsmith gave her statement the other day she assumed that Elinor had been at work that morning, so Elinor would have disappeared somewhere around lunchtime, before she was due to open up the library. Her mother's statement here says she hadn't seen her daughter that morning before she went off to work, as she was already gone when she woke up. But there's an interview here of her supervisor at the Town Council offices. It turns out she wasn't expected in that morning. She had been given most of the morning off, in compensation for a late night opening of the library. It was a new idea; I suppose an early form of flexible working. Elinor doesn't seem to have mentioned it to her mother, but, in her interview, Mrs Sommers says that she had been working flat out on a rush order the night before and hadn't spoken to Elinor. She just assumed she had come in and gone to bed."

"Was Elinor actually home that night?"

Andrew glanced down at the notes. "It doesn't say. Would her mother know if her bed had not been slept in? Elinor was probably trained to make her bed, so there wouldn't have been any difference from one morning to the next, when her mother looked in."

He looked at the older man. "There was one thing I wanted to ask you. What did you mean when you said earlier about the day of her disappearance, if that was the day she died?"

"When I said that, I was just pointing out that there could have been a gap. She may have been hiding somewhere, or..."

"Or kidnapped?" a new train of possibilities had opened for the young policeman.

"That had been the theory I thought we shouldn't rule out, but now we also have the chance that she met her death the night before. Have you looked through all the reports?"

"Not quite, but it's a slim folder. It won't take long. But if we have to extend our investigation to places she may have been hidden then that's some task."

Evans picked up the folder. "When a child vanishes there is usually an appeal for people to check outhouses and places where an accident could have occurred. Ah yes." He selected a sheet of paper. "There was an appeal, but no positive findings."

Andrew updated the board adding the two new possible dates for Elinor's disappearance and death, before joining Davies in reading the documents from 1972.

"I think we should have both Hughes and O'Flaherty in here to take their statements about the dig in 1972." Davies finished reading one paper and handed it to Andrew to read. "We have the original statement from the leader, a Professor Beacham, and both Hughes and O'Flaherty are on the list of students who had left on schedule the day before Elinor was reported missing. Beacham himself had stayed a few extra days to write up reports, settle bills and generally see to the wrapping up of the dig. There's nothing much in his statement. I think the police constable of the time just wanted a list of those who were involved in the dig, in case any links were discovered. I've been in contact with Hughes about the resumption of the dig. Suppose I take him and you interview O'Flaherty?"

Andrew nodded his acceptance and after seeing his superior officer out, locked the door and retired to his own part of the building.

"*Feierabend!* Time to stop work." Matthias closed his notebook decisively and gathered up his papers from the common room table. It started a general. It had been a long week. "What are you all planning for Sunday?" Saturday had been a full day on the site, to make up for the loss of time since the discovery of the body, but it had been decided that Sunday would be a free day. "We have the rest of this evening too. Any suggestions?"

The moon was a silver crescent in a sky that had still been light at eight o'clock that night. Around the moon the sky was a clear blue, like a colour wash that was darkest at its height, then with streaks of pale grey, pinks and purples nearer the horizon. By midnight the tide was in at Kames Bay, as they sat on the rocks to shed their outer clothing and leave it in bundles on the rocks. There was no wind as they ran rapidly into the sea and began swimming vigorously across the bay, where they turned and made their way back to the other side. Still clad in their swim wear, they dried off roughly and scrambled into their clothes.

The firm wet sand of Kames Bay, free of rocks and seaweed, was a good surface for gymnastics. It was fairly kind to the joints and Matthias completed a few training routines, forward and backward flips, double and single hand-stands. Graziella and Kathryn joined in with a few runs of cartwheels, but the others stood by, jogging up and down to regain some warmth, before setting off for the spot where their bikes were parked.

"You are really good." Dean complimented Matthias, as they strolled at a more leisurely pace towards the bikes. "Are you in some kind of gymnastics club?"

"Not any more. I was quite keen at school. Now I just do it because I enjoy it. I became too tall to be top-notch, but it keeps me out of mischief. Studying the classics is pretty sedentary so it's a good counterbalance."

Graziella and Kathryn sped away towards the bikes, leaving Dean and Matthias in their wake.

"Do you believe in love at first sight?" Dean blurted out. It was not a question he would have asked of Markus, Paul or even Connor, but somehow he felt that Matthias would treat the question seriously and not with derision.

"Of course," he replied. "It wasn't how it happened for me, but I think it's too well known to be in any doubt. Everyone is different." When Dean did not venture any further information or comment, he continued. "I have known Elvira since childhood, but it wasn't until I was sixteen that I realised I wanted to spend the rest of my life with her. For you it was different?" His voice rose with the question.

"It's Alice. I don't know if she wants to be more than friends and I don't want to spoil it. I do know she wants a career and I don't know if she'll have time for me." Dean poured out his doubts in a confused jumble. "Are you engaged then?" he asked Matthias.

"Not yet. It will be some time before I am earning, but we can wait. I think Alice will soon let you know how she feels about you," With this reassurance he let the subject drop.

It took them very little time to reach the hot showers of the hostel and when they joined the others, a feeling of well-being and triumph was the mood in the common room.

"That was definitely worth doing, something memorable, as I don't suppose any of us will be making a habit of it," said Kathryn, her fingers wrapped round a mug of hot chocolate.

"We could have been more organised. A *Feuerzangbowle* would have been great now," Markus remarked.

"A what?" Connor asked.

"I suppose the nearest translation would be a hot punch. It's heated red wine, spices and rum. You drip it onto a sugar cone and light it, so that it drips into the punch. Very dramatic. And guaranteed to warm you up."

"Maybe tomorrow? We can get the ingredients here or in Largs."

◆ ◆ ◆

A few miles away, in Millport, Susan opened the deep drawer where she kept her old photographs. Her professional work was meticulously filed and catalogued. But this collection was a hodgepodge of family collections from different eras. Albums of black paper held small sepia-coloured snaps from box brownie cameras. Later albums had specially bought corners to hold the photographs secure. Earlier ones had slanted slits into which the images could be clipped. There were some plastic holders from the 70s, each recording a holiday abroad. But the rest just lay in a pile, layer upon layer of forgotten moments, each witness to a fleeting second where smiles were directed towards the lens, where best clothes were donned for a visit to a studio, where a newly christened child lay on a hand-knitted shawl, both child and shawl proudly displayed for posterity.

She burrowed through the layers of family history. Yes,

here it was. It was one of a pile of those square black and white photographs from the seventies. A crease was stretched diagonally from the top left corner and another marred the surface of the lower half. In the bottom corner, the glazed surface was curling away from the backing layer.

It was one of the thousands taken by the resident photographer in Millport. For years, part of his flourishing business was based on street photography. Every day he snapped pedestrians on the seafront. Next morning the photographs were displayed for sale in his shop window and extra copies could be ordered. Susan's father had his own camera, and Susan herself had received a camera for her thirteenth birthday and yet Susan's family were regular summer customers, buying the photographs that recorded their carefree holiday moments in Millport.

She looked more closely at the first one she had taken out of the drawer and wondered why they had bought this particular one. It was clear that a ferry had just arrived at the old pier. Holiday makers streamed towards the town in the background of the photograph. The main subjects were four figures, her father, an aunt and uncle, a cousin. Possibly it had been purchased because it was a rare shot of her uncle. A keen photographer himself, he was usually at the other side of the lens.

Her memory had not let her down. Elinor was in the next photograph. although not in the foreground. The date stamp showed it had been taken a few days before she had disappeared. The main subjects were her own mother and father, snapped as they passed the bakers at the bottom of the steep hill that led to the parish church, a simple shopping trip memorialised in black and white. Yes, the figure in tennis skirt and sleeveless top was definitely Elinor. Her racquet, frozen into immobility by the camera shutter, would have been swinging nonchalantly at her side.

Susan laid the photograph down with a sigh and picked up the first one again. The scene in this snap was fairly crowded, bearing witness to the increased population of the town in the summer months. Walking up and down the main street was one of the most exciting ways of passing the time, only beaten by watching a boat arrive at the pier. Shopping for food could be a twice daily event in those pre-refrigerator days. Fresh hot breakfast rolls were on sale from seven, or even earlier from the side door of the bakery. Farm milk was poured directly into quart milk cans, brought by the customers. In Millport you could subtract a decade from the calendar date.

Of course this photograph was dated too. Susan turned it over. The back was blank apart from a slightly smudged purple date stamp, made with one of those adjustable devices used by the library used to say when a book was due to be returned. This was a blessing. No one had bothered to write on the back where or when it had been taken. At the time you knew. Afterwards it was too tedious a chore. And then it was too late, the knowledge disappearing as the knowledgeable died.

Susan reached for her strong magnifying light. This photograph was taken later than the other one, in fact on the very day Elinor vanished. The subject might be mundane, but the camera work was excellent. She examined the outline of a smaller figure in the background. Yes, she was right. He had lied; he had been on the island that day.

CUMBRAE 1972

"What are you doing here?" Elinor's clear voice startled him and he swung round, eyes wide. All his planning had been destroyed by one moment of carelessness.

He had not meant to push her, only brush her out of the way, prevent her from seeing too much. But he overestimated the force needed to shove her aside. Elinor was slightly built and her footing on the uneven ground was precarious.

She had been startled when his head had appeared, as he made his way up the steep hillside path and surprise turned to alarm when she saw the gleaming blade of the two edged sword. She had been about to descend the narrow footpath to the shore thirty yards below. Although it was not wide, she had used it hundreds of times in perfect safety. There was just room for a faster walker to overtake another, or for two people to pass, as long as one was prepared to step aside into the undergrowth that obtruded on each side.

He had no time to conceal the sword, the last item from the hoard, the one that had needed extra planning to transport to a new hiding place. In his heightened state of excitement, he had not been thinking straight. He should have resisted the temptation to remove the sword from his backpack to test it on the tendrils of greenery that lined the path. He had been stupid, more than stupid in that the condition of the sword would affect its value. But he had never seriously tried to suppress his reckless streak. And now it was his downfall. If Elinor had stumbled to the right, landward, all might still have been well. But she fell towards the sea and he looked in horror as her body landed in the bracken below. As he scrambled down the path in panic, he still had a desperate hope that all might be well. Bracken is soft and springy, he thought frantically. It will have broken her fall.

But the hope was in vain. The rocks of Cumbrae had claimed a victim. When he reached Elinor she was lying face up, but her head had come to rest on a rock and he could see the blood that had pooled around the now lifeless body.

There was no good logical reason for what he did next. If Elinor's body had been found where it lay, the chances were that her death would have been declared an unfortunate accident and there would have been the usual calls for additional safety measures, or warning signs, to protect the unwary. But O'Flaherty feared that some trace of his involvement remained, that his part in her death would be discovered.

It was tragically easy to lift her body to a place nearby, where it would be easily concealed and later to carry it under cover of darkness to the dig site, where there was little trace of the dig that had taken place. Although the trenches had been re-filled, the turf had not been replaced yet. The soil was still soft from the careful sieving. He would be able to reopen one trench to an adequate depth, lay the body in and scoop the earth back over it. Tomorrow he would be miles away and the evidence of his crime would be concealed for ever.

The hoard he had discovered, removed and concealed had been a curious mixture. Amongst a clutch of coins, he had seen many silver Scottish silver pennies from the time of Alexander III. One had been pierced as if it had been used as a pendant or a brooch rather than currency. The cross on the reverse side meant that it would have been appropriate as a holy medal, a theory all the more likely as the coin had been altered; indentations symbolising the wounds of Christ had been worked around the cross, where jewels had once been set, although these had disappeared. The rest of the jewellery however was undoubtedly Norse, similar to finds elsewhere in burial sites; a gold clasp, earrings, a necklace, the collection of a single person, but one wealthy enough to have owned such trinkets.

The sword was the glory of the haul. Light in weight and made of flexible steel, it was typical of the swords carried by knights in the thirteenth century. On each side of the blade, two grooves ran from the finely honed tip to the hilt. It would withstand the fiercest fighting and, if wielded by a strong warrior, would be quite capable of splitting a skull in two. But the inscription was what intrigued him most. Inlaid in gold wire along one side of the blade was an inscription in no language he had ever seen. At each side was a cross and then a single run of letters. The pommel, hilt and the letters suggested a Viking owner, though the sword could have been made elsewhere. Its discovery would spark interest worldwide, if it were made public. Kept secret it could raise enough from a private collector to make him a wealthy man.

The decision had not taken him long. Wealth was more enticing than whatever plaudits the academic world might deliver, especially given his deviousness in not announcing the discovery immediately. It was too late to fake a discovery. His plan had been to carry away part of the treasure, but to leave the sword and the rest of the hoard well-hidden, depart as scheduled and later return unobtrusively to retrieve the treasures and gradually sell the items.

The original hiding place was as convenient a spot as any to conceal his haul. It had after all successfully housed the treasure for centuries. The space was narrow and dark, little light filtering in through the undergrowth above. A concave shelf, a little above head height, was deep enough to hold his long thin bundle till he came back for it.

He was confident that his return had been equally skilfully accomplished. The danger had lasted only from when he strode up the gangway of the last ferry of the day, up the first narrow street and along the coast road. He had a sleeping bag in his rucksack as he intended to sleep out, retrieve the treasure and travel home the next day.

Now everything had changed. His final act, before setting out for the ferry, was to replace the sword back on the shelf where it had lain for centuries.

CUMBRAE 2005

A free Sunday offered a chance of a sight-seeing trip to Glasgow or even to Edinburgh, though the distance would mean a very short time in the capital. O'Flaherty had told them he would be crossing to Largs and would be happy to spare a half hour or so to show anyone interested the possible sites of the Battle of Largs or just to give them a map and directions if they wished to explore themselves. In the event no-one opted to go any further afield than Largs and only Connor, Paul and Dean and Kathryn took up the battle site tour, although Matthias and Alice accompanied them on the ferry to Largs for a foray to the big Largs supermarket to get the ingredients for that night's hot punch.

Graziella and Markus, back on Cumbrae, stood in front of the rock face and examined it speculatively.

"I have done some artificial climbing walls, just for fun," Graziella said. "In fact our local fire brigade has converted one side of their building into a wall for young people and run competitions in the summer evenings while the parents and grandparents sit at the cafes drinking wine and looking on. Mostly it's for schoolkids, though.

"I expect, too, they use ropes and safety harnesses. One of the challenges of bouldering is to do it without ropes, although helmets and safety is important. Despite anything my brother says, I'm not reckless."

"Our local peaks are for serious alpinists only. Ice axes,

ropes, crampons and so on. I'd like to try something in between."

Markus unslung a small backpack and shook out a pair of
climbing shoes. "You don't really need these, but they do help.
The tip is shaped to help you grip onto the rock. Artificial walls
are usually cement with plastic holds. This is natural sandstone
so we have to plan our own route up, finding holds. Fancy a go?"

As they walked they assessed the rock formations, but
there were very few that offered the possibility of a climb. Most
of the ground sloped down, with scrub and fern growing out and
covering the surface.

"What about there?" Graziella pointed to a rock where
the two sandstone fissures overlapped, their outline sharp and
clean. They faced a small bay where the high tide covered most
of the sandy beach, protruding rocks to either side forming a
natural breakwater. There was no-one in sight, but an inflatable
rubber motor boat rocked on the gentle waves, very near the
shore, its anchor cast over the side.

To reach the rocks they needed to cross some rough
ground, where small flags of bog cotton showed that the ground
could easily become marshy in damper conditions. Now it was
dry and easily traversed. The lush ferns were cracked to form a
narrow path, perhaps the run to some animal's den.

Markus surveyed the surface dubiously. "Not much good.
In fact, not any good," he waved his hand dismissively at the
smooth outcrop as Graziella stopped beside him.

But this is interesting." She peered curiously at a cleft that
had been formed by a split in the stone. It had been imper-
ceptible from the road, but it was wide enough to go inside. "It
isn't a cave, because you can see the sky through the leaves, but
it gets too narrow to climb."

Markus joined her and looked upwards. The light was dim,
filtered by a screen of vegetation but he could see a darker line
just above head height. It was the work of a moment to reach
it. His bent knee brought his left foot up to feel along the stone
for a narrow hold and his right hand easily found the edge of a

ledge more than wide enough for him to clench his fist over it securely and raise his head to squint into the gloomy niche.

"There's something here!" he said.

With both feet and one hand securely gripping the rock, Markus was able to reach in with his right hand and distinguish a hard circular item amongst the fragments of broken rock. He managed to grasp it and transfer it to his pocket, but his position was too precarious to do a complete search. Lithely he made his way to the ground and held a small metal object out to Graziella.

"It's money. Is this all of it?"

Markus shrugged. "It would be better with a torch and a bit more height, but I felt right along the shelf and as far as I know there is just this single coin."

LARGS 2005

It was not man's power which drove him away, but the power of God which crushed his ships.

Melrose Chronicle

A magic-raised watery tempest blew upon our warriors, ambitious of conquest, and against the floating habitations of the brave. The roaring billows and stormy blast threw shielded companies of our adventurous nation on the Scottish strand.

Sturla Þórðarson, Norwegian account of Haco's expedition against Scotland,

A few minutes from the ferry slipway there was a municipal car park where O'Flaherty had arranged to meet his small group. They found him waiting there, standing nonchalantly beside an impressive motor bike, talking to a group of bikers who had also parked there.

When he saw the trio arrive, he drew off his leather gauntlets and stowed them in the bike's pannier before making his way over.

"We are going south to where the Gogo burn flows into the Clyde, but, if you have time later, the Vikingar centre just a short way along there is worth a visit, as is the Art Deco Italian cafe you pass on the way." He gestured in the other direction before leading them along the promenade. Across the firth they could see the area on Cumbrae where their dig was.

"This is commonly recognised as the spot where the fighting took place. Largs did have a castle, probably no more than a simple fortress, further uphill. But, in an area where space between the heights and the sea is limited, this was an obvious place for the Scots to attack the invaders. The first Norse to come ashore on the mainland of Scotland at Largs did so unwillingly. Five vessels were forced aground by the fierce winds against which their oars were powerless. At sea, crews of the larger transport vessels fought desperately to prevent the same fate befalling their vessels. On Cumbrae, Haakon watched in despair as his treasure ship was driven nearer and nearer the Scottish mainland. If you look up, you will see the height advantage that the Scots had. The Scots' first attack on those Norsemen stranded on the shore was with missiles. Arrows and slingshot wounded many, as they sheltered behind their beached boats, but few were killed at this point in the conflict.

"When the fighting came, it was fierce and bloody on both sides. The Scots had the advantage of trained cavalry when it was possible to use them. They also had commanders who could direct the forces. The Norsemen and their allies were rightly feared as formidable foes, but they fought under many leaders and without a co-ordinated plan. When Haakon himself led the counter attack, the Scots retired."

He consulted an index card that he produced from his pocket, "Later, Ogmund Krækidants, Andrew Nicolson, Erling Alfson, Andrew Pott, Ronald Urka, Thorlaug Bosi, and Paul Soor were left in command with about nine hundred men, while Haakon was persuaded to withdraw to Cumbrae to fetch reinforcements.

"Outnumbered by the well-armed Scots they were driven back, with multiple losses. They attempted to retreat in good order, but this was misunderstood by those manning the boats on the beach and many pushed off, leaving the stranded men to fight a desperate rear-guard action on the beach. Individual acts of bravery drew admiration. The Scots knight, Fergus, was slain by Andrew Nicolson, who took his knight's belt as a trophy. As the Norsemen took to their boats the Scots drew off uphill.

"Next morning the Norsemen collected their dead without challenge, but could not determine how many Scots had been killed, as their bodies had already been carried off. The Scots expected to fight on. The storm was losing force and Haakon had many men and many ships to replace the ones lost, their shallow drafts easily able to beach in the shelving bay.

"Five days later they were gone. The threat was over."

Dr O'Flaherty sketched out a salute. It had been an impressive performance, delivered with full dramatic effect. "I'll leave you to your own devices and see you at our first session tomorrow morning." Instead of retracing his steps along the promenade he headed for the high street and disappeared from view.

CUMBRAE 2005

That evening, Alice discovered that O'Flaherty's street credibility had shot up, not by any impressive exposition of the Battle of Largs, but by his possession of a highly enviable BMW bike.

"An R1200 GS," said an awestruck Connor. "It's only been on the market a year."

"Expensive, is it?" Kathryn asked.

"I expect you could get a small house in Millport for less."

"It's cutting edge technology. Good for both off-road and touring. The last models were built for off road and were heavy and cumbersome. These ones are much lighter, about 30 kilos."

Connor had too many of the bike's specifications at his fingertips to retain his audience and the group split, according to the degree of interest in the finer details of gearboxes and cam shafts.

"No axle? You don't say." Alice's sarcasm was lost on them. Even Matthias, the stalwart advocate of traditional locomotion, of using feet to travel on level ground, was sucked into the enthusiastic admiration for the versatility of the machine.

"He's bringing it over on the ferry, to have it handy when the course ends."

"He'd be healthier sticking to pedalling. All that beer consumption is telling." It was a mean remark, but Alice could not eradicate a deep-seated dislike of the man.

"Who knows what we'll be like in thirty years." Graziella

sighed. "My mama was gorgeous, curvy yet so slim. Now, well, she has more of everything. But she just tells my papa he should be grateful."

"It's one of the ironies that, when you see groups of motor-cyclist, the majority are middle-aged."

The supermarket in Largs had furnished the ingredients for the hot punch that was to be made before the meeting they were holding after supper to discuss their progress in investigating Elinor's death.

It says much for the good relationship that the group had forged with Mrs Macbeth that she had been prepared to take the evening off and give them the run of her normally jealously guarded kitchen. She had prepared the meal as far as she could, the cock-a-leekie soup was simmering very gently on the hob of the Aga stove, while the various ovens held pots of tiny Ayrshire potatoes and a rich stew of Aberdeen Angus beef. The fridge held two large bowls of cranachan and a separate bowl of raspberries for topping. All that they needed to do was to serve up. When she had heard their plans, she had even added a clootie dumpling as an accompaniment to the Feuerzangbowle, "to soak up all that alcohol." It came as no surprise, however, that she discovered it intact the next morning, when it became part of that day's packed lunch.

"Wow. I won't need to eat for a month." Graziella sat back and surveyed the others, who looked just as replete, swallowed the last spoonful of cranachan, savouring the taste of raspberry, cream and honey.

"No room for the Feuerzangbowle?"

"After a break, I might manage a couple of sips. When does the demonstration take place?"

"Eight o'clock." Markus looked at his brother speculatively. "Time for a run?"

"Probably."

Clearing up was done in record time, especially as Mrs Macbeth had issued dire warnings against trying to load or run the dishwasher.

"Fine. Our meeting will start at eight thirty." Kathryn had been setting up the common room and was now ready for a short jogging session. Everyone took some part, a few content to turn back at the Lion Rock, while Paul displayed a hitherto concealed talent for running,

"Compulsory cross-country hare and hounds runs; they were hell, but the easiest way was to get it over as quickly as possible," he panted as he tried to match Matthias stride for stride.

By the time they reached the hostel again Markus was in the kitchen surrounded by the others, engaged in slicing oranges and lemons; Alice, grateful to discover that the red wine had screw tops rather than corks, put it into a large pot to heat gently on the simmer plate of the stove.

"We got sugar cubes," Kathryn observed. "You said that would do."

"Mm, traditionally you have a sugar cone and a special holder with slots to let the sugar and rum liquid drip through, but we can improvise. We need a wire holder. Connor wouldn't sacrifice any of his precious banjo strings, but he promised to come up with something that will do as a substitute."

The rum ignited successfully and the flaming sugar melted and dripped dramatically through the makeshift holder. Soon they were able to move through to the common room clutching their warm mugs.

Kathryn set up the easel and flipchart, as they settled down to sip the hot punch appreciatively. She had already written in some headings and prompts. Under suspects, motives, opportunity she had listed additional possibilities: personal animosity; someone jealous of Elinor, annoyed with something she had done or not done; something dangerous she had found out, like her boss fiddling the books.

"I want to lay to rest the theory that Susan Clearsmith was involved," Alice said with some heat. "And not just because she has a cute dog." She glared balefully at Connor, who had been ill-advised enough to repeat the remark that Matthias had made in the cafe. "It just doesn't make sense. There isn't a shred of credible motive. Life was going well for Susan. The friendship with Elinor was always a 'summer' thing. She was moving on."

"I'm inclined to agree. I'm not so sure about Tom Forrest though." Kathryn, perched on the table beside the flip chart, looked at her list of tentative suspects. "Who knows how close they were? He seems to have been a local heart throb. Maybe Elinor was too clingy. Maybe they had an affair that to him was just a casual encounter, but that she thought was the start of a serious relationship."

"That man, Mr Gordon, smoked a pipe too. He's my choice." Dean had decided to dismiss Tom as a suspect. When Tom had come to Dean's rescue after the tent collapsed, there was no hint of a troubled man who was returning to the scene of his crime. There had, however, been something unsettling in how Sandy Gordon had caressed the Viking weapons he had brought to the hostel to show them.

"Most people are killed by someone they know. She and Sandy had been in the same school class for most of their lives. He could have been infatuated by Elinor and his passions inflamed when she spurned him."

"Hard to imagine. I'll have to take your word for it." Connor observed. "I've never had any trouble. Lots of women find me appealing."

"Your aunties and grannies don't count."

Paul's riposte failed to squash Connor, but drew amused smiles from the others. The investigative part of the evening petered out as glasses were refilled and Connor's strumming on his banjo provided the background for general conversation.

The single silver coin that Markus had found remained forgotten in his pocket for the present.

CUMBRAE 1263

On the third day after the battle Ragnhild watched from the highest point on Cumbrae, as her father's flagship departed. At dawn a light haze had covered land and sea, so she saw the gilded prow through a veil of mist as it sailed the length of Cumbrae and slipped round the Mull of Kintyre to start its long journey north to Bergen. The rest of the fleet departed in stages.

The sunset that night was glorious. The clouds were lit by a rosy glow and, where they were grey, this had been turned to a purple sheen. They sat unmoving in the sky, like islands in a light blue sea, fingers of clouds forming fiords, rivulets and reefs. Even to those who were used to seeing the northern lights the western Scottish sky was magnificent and the splendour intensified in the afterglow of the setting sun, when the fiery red and grey stripes outshone the sails of the retreating ships.

Even before the tempest that had been decisive in the conflict, the talk in the Norwegian fleet had been that Haakon had lost the willpower to continue. His loyal captains worried about his health; his less committed allies turned their thoughts to the possibility of placating King Alexander and changing sides.

It was almost a year before Ragnhild learned that her father had not survived long enough to reach Norway. He had fallen ill and died in Orkney and his final voyage had been from there to his burial vault in Bergen Cathedral. Haakon's raven banner would never again appear in the waters of the Clyde.

Magnus was now king and it might have been possible to return, but, as Ragnhild caressed the baby, warmly wrapped in her woollen shawl, she knew that Cumbrae was now home. The islanders lived simply and she and Harald had become part of the community. Stone was available in abundance to build stout walls that kept out wind and rain, with heather and turf for roofing. Wood was scarcer, something that Ragnhild, born in a land of forests, found strange. But they had a home, built like the others on the island, basic, simple, warm and redolent of the fragrances of herbs.

Fishing was done from small vessels and at first they were able to use one in exchange for part of their catch until they had saved enough to be able to afford one of their own, without dipping into the precious resources they had packed in Bergen what now seemed a lifetime ago. Harald's strength and skill was welcome as crew when the islanders' ships ventured into deeper water and this too helped them to build a simple home for their little family.

Although Ragnhild had hated her needle, she had been much more interested in making cloth. Now she was glad that her mother had ensured that she could spin too. To Margarete, it was an important womanly skill. But she had liked it less when Ragnhild had shown an interest in how to dye wool and linen. The queen was content to have the skeins of yarn brought to her so that she could select the best colours for her work. Ragnhild liked to visit the dyers, peer into their caldrons and handle the plants they used. She was fascinated by the processes by which colour was obtained, but Margarete frowned upon her dye-stained fingers, so unbecoming in a royal princess.

Now, on Cumbrae, she made dyes and healing potions from plants and heather honey, which added to their income, but also gained her the respect and gratitude of the islanders, whose tongue she was finding easier as time went on.

In Bergen they had been used to the sound of many languages, as seafarers from many countries visited to trade. The lyrics of French troubadours had been carried to Norway by returning crusaders. From Magister William, Harald had learned a smattering of English, which bore some similarity to the Scots language. Haakon's links to the Western Isles and Ireland had drawn bards whose Gaelic songs had always been well received in Norwegian halls. Now Harald's music enriched the lives of the is-

landers.

CUMBRAE 2005

D ai Evans regarded the young police constable with sympathy. He could understand how the news he had just broken would have disappointed the eager young man.

"I'm sorry, but that's it. The decision is from higher up. The case is not closed, but I'm off it. I have to head back later today. It's a matter of budgeting and priorities. It has been good experience for you, but this case isn't likely to be solved quickly."

"If it isn't closed, I can carry on?" Andrew MacGillivray had impressed Evans by how he had taken the news. It was hard to avoid getting emotionally involved in cases, but vital if you were to do your job properly.

"Of course, but it mustn't be allowed to interfere with your normal duties. The truth may emerge sooner or later. Who knows? Meanwhile take tomorrow off. You'll be all the better for a break and come back able to look at things afresh. That's an order."

Andrew accepted the truth of the more experienced man's views and was glad that the decision had been taken out of his hands. He would take tomorrow off and get in a spot of fishing at the reservoir.

Tuesday morning found him, therefore, unknowingly retracing the footsteps of Elinor's last journey until he branched off to the two artificial stretches of water that served the island. And he was unreachable when events reached a dramatic climax.

Booths in pubs allowed for a degree of privacy but it was deceptive. It often led to the assumption that, in each pod, people were busy with their own conversations and that no-one nearby was listening. O'Flaherty sat alone with his midday pint in the farthest booth; no-one had to pass him to reach their booth and Tom and Susan chose the next booth without even realising there was someone within earshot, as Susan described her significant find.

"According to Dr O'Flaherty he was off the island. But I think I can disprove that. They finished at the dig the day before and they all left on the same ferry. They were both interviewed by the police and the other one, the professor, was with O'Flaherty as far as Glasgow, so he corroborates the story. The problem is that I've found an old photograph that definitely puts O'Flaherty on the island the next day at the old pier, though he could be coming back off the ferry."

"That's just yards from Elinor's house," Tom interjected.

In the neighbouring booth O'Flaherty shrugged dismissively. To the best of his knowledge he had not set eyes on Elinor before their fatal meeting and had no idea where she had lived.

Susan too was unsure of the relevance of this proximity to Elinor's home. She was quite certain that no casual assignation figured in Elinor's fate; it didn't tally with all she knew of her personality.

"Well I have promised to take Alice up to the Glaid Stone when she's finished at the museum. I looked in at the police station but there's just a notice with Andrew's mobile number for emergencies. This has waited years, so there's no point in spoiling his time off. I thought I'd pop round later and let him see what he thinks of the photograph."

O'Flaherty waited till the couple had departed before emerging from the pub. He was all too aware that his heart was beating rapidly and sweat had gathered on his brow, despite the cool breeze that was blowing. He knew he would have to take action. Fast.

His first plan was to skulk around the area near the police station, wait till Susan appeared and somehow waylay her to seize the photograph that could damn him. Then stories of motor cycle theft sprang to mind, thieves speeding off after snatching handbags in streets crowded with unwary tourists. Adopting this method would mean he could act more quickly, no need to wait till Susan was on her way to the police station. Thanks to his eavesdropping he knew her plans for the afternoon and it would be the work of a moment to gain possession of her bag and its damning contents. It was the only chance of his part in Elinor's death remaining unproved. The panniers of his bike were already packed for a rapid departure from the island.

His over-confidence blinded him to the flaws in his plans. But he knew that his decision was a life changing one. His academic career would be over and he would have to reinvent himself, choose a new lifestyle. Money was not a problem; his profits from the original haul had been considerable and what remained would be ample for his future needs. He had no emotional baggage; any relationships had been brief; no friendships had been deep, just alcohol-fuelled acquaintanceships cultivated in bars and hostelries.

In the event Montmorency proudly led a fair-sized group up past the Cathedral on the way to the stone that marked the highest point of the island. His joy expressed itself in scampering ahead and returning to run round the group.

"You would think he was a sheepdog," said Graziella as she felt him brush past her legs.

"If you wait till he is up at the heather, you'll see him forget all about us. When he gets the scent of rabbit, he is all West

Highland terrier."

Despite being on the island for a week, most of the students had not walked to the top of the island and when Alice had mentioned her plans the idea had caught on. Kathryn and Paul chose to cycle and take the more gradual route, meeting them at the top. This also meant Kathryn could do a little shopping for presents beforehand. Connor promised vaguely either to catch up or meet them on the way down, depending on his progress with his latest lyrics.

The heather was in full bloom, carpeting the ground in blazing purple, though there were some sprigs of white heather to be found, traditionally associated with good luck. As they rounded the curve past the road that led to the little cottage hospital the incline became steeper.

"The Lady Margaret Hospital," Alice read. "Another Margaret. There are so many in our story too: the wife of our King Haakon, the wife of King Alexander, daughters and granddaughters. The sagas are impossible. Nearly every man is called Haakon or Harald. Females are Margarete, Christina, or Ragnhild."

"I think I prefer the traditional approach. You would too, if you had been lumbered with a name like Dean."

"You could always change it to Alexander." Matthias suggested, swishing the tall grass at the side of the road with his foot.

"This Margaret would appeal to you, Alice," Susan continued, pointing across to the island of Bute, whose coastline had become visible, particularly when there were breaks in the dry stone wall on the west side of the road "She lived just across there and was the only daughter of the third Marquis of Bute, who owned Cumbrae in the nineteenth century. He was a strong believer in female education. Margaret was taught Greek and her father had a ceiling in Mount Stuart House specially painted with the portraits of more than a hundred female heroines, so that she had these to look up to, literally."

When they neared the summit, a small path led off to the

west at the top of which was a metal map, just yards from the concrete pillar of the triangulation point used for mapping the contours of Ordnance Survey maps. Beside it, the Glaid Stone was imposing, an immense sandstone boulder deposited at the summit during the Ice Age.

"The highest point is just over four hundred feet, under a hundred and thirty metres, so it isn't a great height by Scottish standards, but it has a view second to none." Susan was not surprised that cameras had been produced and her offer to take group and individual photographs was enthusiastically taken up. "The map has arrows pointing out the places that can be seen in every compass direction."

Surrounded by spectacular scenery, there was no reason for them to pay any attention to the scanty traffic on the road. Occasional cars passed but no-one stopped in the small parking area and no other walkers arrived. When O'Flaherty drew up on the road below, they were too engrossed to notice.

Bitterly he cursed his bad luck in arriving too late to catch Susan while she was still on the road. He had expected, too, that she would be accompanied only by Alice, not protected by a veritable schiltron. His view was limited as the students moved around the Glaid Stone, but he could see that there was no hope of preserving his anonymity. That this had always been a pipe dream was something he was unable to grasp in his present state of mind, where clear thinking had been replaced by wild recklessness.

With grim determination he dismounted and undid the zip of the fishing rod holder that he had purchased to hold the sword safely and discreetly on his motorbike, when transporting it from the island. He had already decided on brute force when he planned the bag snatch. Now it would be face on. He made his way rapidly up the path towards Susan.

"Give me that photograph," O'Flaherty snarled. For a brief moment Susan saw the humour of the situation. Was O'Flaherty such a technological dinosaur that he really believed the snap, tucked away in her back pack, was the only copy of the incriminating evidence? Had he never heard of scanners, photocopiers, even negatives?

But there was nothing comic about the sword he was brandishing, or the manic violence evident in his face as he held them at bay. The terrain around the Glaid Stone was not ideal for a skirmish: narrow paths ran though the heather in various directions, leading to precipitous ground, where a cliff face dropped to the shore. Overhead gulls wheeled and cried, swooping towards the lochan, where they had nests to protect.

The young people had indeed gathered defensively around Susan. They were standing on the broadest path, blocking his escape towards the road. Although they lacked the shields and pikes of medieval Scottish warriors, they stared unwaveringly at her leather-clad aggressor.

"Why did you kill Elinor?" Alice hoped the question would distract him and buy them time. Didn't murderers like to confess? They did in lots of crime thrillers. She was reassured when he glanced briefly in her direction before replying.

"I didn't kill her. At least I did cause her death, but it was an accident. The path was too narrow and she fell over the edge. When I reached her she was dead." His eyes had rested on Alice for less than a second. His vigilance was unchanged as he checked the others for any sign of movement.

Ringed by his pursuers, O'Flaherty was trapped, but he could kill again. His eyes scanned the group desperately, darting from one to the other, looking for a weak spot through which he could escape. Equally desperately Alice tried to reason with him.

"Look," she said, fixing her eyes on the man's face, rather than the murderous sword he was brandishing, "If what you say is true, Elinor's death was an accident. It wouldn't be murder, manslaughter at the worst." Damn, she thought, not the brightest thing to mention in the circumstances. "You were young; you just panicked. Forensics could help you prove it."

O'Flaherty hesitated a moment, but he was still on guard, his eyes vigilant, checking his antagonists. It was one against six, but the terrain did not lend itself to taking advantage of their numerical superiority. Montmorency growled menacingly, straining at the leash that Susan held tightly.

But in that brief time, when he and Alice had fixed their gaze on one another, the hands of Marcus had moved rapidly, his signal acknowledged by a quick nod from his twin.

When it came, the vault was explosive and dramatic. Matthias cleared the slim pillar of the triangulation station that marked the highest point on the island, flipped into a handstand on the oblong table that held the etched map of the area surrounding Cumbrae and struck out at O'Flaherty's right shoulder with one foot. The sword described an arc and landed in the springy heather, where it was retrieved by Alice.

Disarmed, O'Flaherty tried to run, hampered by the height of the heather. Dean's rugby tackle might have caught him, but he was equally hampered, while fear lent O'Flaherty the speed to reach the motor cycle he had parked at the roadside. One kick at the starter brought it to life and minutes later the sound faded, as he descended the road at full speed.

Kathryn and Paul, cycling uphill, passed him without realising they were witnessing a dramatic escape. In the small bay the hired rigid inflatable boat waited, easily able to hold both him and his motor bike. Within minutes he had gone, travelling swiftly over the choppy water, a small speck that grew ever smaller.

"What I find amazing is how you two were able to act together. It was your arm movement that distracted O'Flaherty, just as Matt started his vault. How could you have done that without talking?"

"Extra-sensory perception," answered Matthias solemnly. "It's a twin thing."

"Quatsch!" his brother countered." Don't be taken in by his rubbish. You deserve to know the truth." He looked at Matthias for consent before continuing.

"All his life Matt has been what my grandmother used to call *'dull of hearing.'* It isn't severe, but he does use lip reading a bit. It's really useful sometimes, as he can tell us what people are saying when we can't hear them. Since we were young he could lip-read anything I just mouthed, but I'm useless at it, so I couldn't read his reply. The solution was to learn sign language." He grinned. "That was mostly so we could talk in class without making any noise."

"We've got a few good routines, too, where we persuade people we can read each other's minds."

"Though sometimes we can." Markus threw out a smiling challenge to their scepticism.

The sword had been delivered to the police station for possible forensic examination, the most dramatic entry ever into the lost and found book. Already the discovery of the double-edged sword was causing excitement in archaeological circles. It was a high status thirteenth century weapon, with an inscription inlaid in gold wire along the blade. Such inscriptions were highly popular at the time, but many are indecipherable, letter combinations that are part contractions, part Latin, part symbol. It had most likely been made in Germany, but the form of some of the letters had Scandinavian features.

"As an artefact I can accept it is beautiful," Alice said. "But when you have seen it being wielded aggressively, you start to understand the ugliness of violence and warfare, rather than the romance that films, stories and paintings convey." She shuddered. "I shall never forget that whirling blade."

At rest, the blade inscription could be seen but its significance was unclear, the run of letters +NDXOXCHWDRGHDX-ORVI+ was some kind of code that so far had eluded them. Alice noted four in particular that contained the letters of the name Ragnhild in the correct order. This might be pure coincidence, but she was convinced there was a story behind it, as yet undiscovered.

Belatedly the third find of the project was produced.

"I am sorry," Markus said, as he produced the coin for Professor Hughes' examination. "We found it yesterday, when we were looking for a spot to do a little climbing, but in all the excitement I totally forgot it. It looks old."

Hughes examined the coin curiously, glad of the distraction. There had been little he could say, when he met the group that morning; he was still coming to terms with the part his colleague had played in the tragic events thirty years ago and also his audacity and shamelessness in the latest developments. It was hard to believe that while he was writing an assessment of the project in the tranquil grounds of the Cathedral, its joint leader was menacing the participants with a lethal weapon.

"This I can identify," he told them, taking the magnifying jeweller's loupe from his eye." I can't claim to be an expert numismatologist but recognition of coins is an important feature of dating archaeological sites. This is a thirteenth century coin."

"Part of Haakon's treasure, perhaps?" Alice speculated.

"Perhaps, but this is a Scottish coin, a silver penny, not particularly rare, but valuable to collectors."

"If you look at this side you'll see the head of Alexander III, complete with crown and sceptre and the inscription Alexander Rex Scotorum, Alexander, King of Scots," He passed it round for them to examine.

"So this is Haakon's opponent. It must have riled Haakon to be defeated by him." Paul examined King Alexander's features with interest.

"It's good to know that the fighting was abandoned in favour of diplomacy. Personally, I see no point in warfare and I'd rather use my medical skills to cure disease than patch up war wounds." Markus spoke with unwonted seriousness.

"Diplomacy, bolstered by financial agreements." Alice pointed out. "Arranged marriages of infant boys and girls, with vast dowries to seal the deal."

"How much was this one worth?" Kathryn hefted the coin in her hand, although the weight was negligible.

"In terms of its purchasing power at the time, I'm afraid I can't say without looking it up, but Alexander's reign is noted for its production of coins. He had several mints across Scotland. Some of the coins raise goodly sums at auction."

"I suppose it depended on the weight of the silver."

"Very much so. If you examine the cross on the obverse side, you'll see that, apart from its use as a Christian symbol, sometimes coins were split in four, the original farthings."

"So, even if it was part of a larger hoard, it's not necessarily evidence of the Norse on Cumbrae?"

"Not definitively, although Haakon's treasure would undoubtedly have contained some of these coins." Hughes was on familiar ground. "Haakon was collecting tribute all the way down the west coast. These Scottish pennies have been found in hoards in England and Belgium. The literature on the subject is vast. Still we shall add it to our records, using all the procedures you have learned; photograph, weigh and measure it. But how and why it got where you found it remains a mystery, a matter for conjecture."

"That's what appeals to me about archaeology," Connor was in a thoughtful mood as he turned the coin around in his hand. This wee bit of silver has a history linked to many people down through the centuries, meaning perhaps a lot to one person, or virtually irrelevant to someone whose wealth was counted in gold.

CUMBRAE 1972

F inding the hidden hoard had taken no skill or expertise. Like the finding of the Dead Sea scrolls or the cave paintings at Lascaux, it had been sheer luck. O'Flaherty had not been a particularly assiduous worker on the dig, finding the labour tedious, and so he had taken to avoiding what he considered drudgery, whenever the opportunity presented itself. One successful ploy had been his offer to provide some sketches of the Isle of Bute from the Cumbrae coast since it played a significant part in the story. The drawings were far more quickly produced than the time he spent away from the dig and he supplemented them by desultory sketches of the coves and rock faces, becoming far more interested in these than historical research.

One shadow on the cliff face had intrigued him. No natural mark on the stone would account for it. He left the little bay, where he had been quite happily doing nothing, and made his way towards what he discovered was a narrow crevice wide enough at the entrance but soon tapering to nothing where the rock was solid. The walls were rough and just above head height there was another split. As a pipe smoker he carried matches, but also a supply of wooden spills, for when the pipe refused to light quickly. These gave some more illumination for his search.

A fragment of what looked like leather protruded from the shelf, showing that he was not the first to discover this niche. A few leaps were needed before his fingers closed on the material and brought a cascade of small metal pieces that tumbled down, like a payout from a one-armed bandit. The haul from an ancient robbery had fallen into the hands of someone almost equally unscrupulous as Rudri of Bute.

Not for one minute did he consider revealing his find openly and becoming entangled in the laws of treasure trove. His definition of right and wrong had always been skewed by his own self-interest. It took some time and more visits before he was able to assess the extent of the treasure, but his decision to exploit it for his own profit was made instantly. Cleverly used, it should provide him with a private income that would free him from the burden to do any work he found tedious. All that he needed now was a plan to transport it to a place where he could safely retrieve items as and when he desired. An academic career would supply a basic income and a pension. His discovery would provide the luxuries.

CUMBRAE 2005

"There is something I still don't understand." Graziella shot Markus a grin, well aware that the question was often asked at the conclusion of a mystery story. "Why did he not just take the treasure and go? Why all the fiasco of hiding it and coming back for it? Why the subterfuge? She glanced at Paul. "In case you are astonished at my wide vocabulary, fiasco and subterfuge are the same, or almost the same in Italian."

Paul refused the challenge. He had his own question.

"Why did he go to all the trouble of hiding Elinor's body? If we believe his version of the story and she fell, he could just have left her there, where she would in all likelihood have been discovered and her death put down as a tragic accident, which according to him it was."

"Remorse?" There was a question in Connor's voice. "Perhaps he couldn't square it with some deep instinct within him, just to leave her body exposed to the elements. He felt compelled to give her some sort of burial?"

"Not remorseful enough to confess and face all the questions about what he was doing back on the island. If he had reported her death she would have been buried properly and her poor mother would have been saved the heartache of never knowing, for the rest of her life, what had happened to her daughter." Alice was not prepared to spare O'Flaherty any sympathy, far less forgiveness.

"He may have been contrite." Graziella, as ever, was more prepared to be generous. "Protecting his hoard had cost a life. Perhaps he wasn't so sunk in villainy that he could complete the deed, but moral cowardice prevented him from confessing."

"And yet he was prepared to be part of a dig so near where he had buried the body. That's foolhardy." Kathryn shared the general puzzlement that O'Flaherty had taken this risk.

"Another character trait," Markus observed. "He thrives on danger, riding a fast bike, rock climbing when he was younger. I think he was reckless but also arrogant. He knew the dig would take place and thought if he participated he could ensure the trenches were placed to avoid the burial spot."

"Aye well we know how that turned out." Dean knew he would never forget his own part in the discovery of Elinor's pathetic remains. "That sword isn't something you could pack easily, but I suspect he managed to get quite a good haul and who knows what has become of it."

CUMBRAE 1972
(AND AFTER)

Minutes away from Glasgow Central Station there was a choice of banks, each housed in an imposing Victorian building and offering a variety of sizes of safe deposit boxes for a modest annual fee. When their train came to a halt, O'Flaherty made his way under the departure and arrivals board that guided the thousands of daily passengers on their chosen journeys. His backpack was heavy, but not large and, without the sword, a medium sized box would be sufficient for his needs. With some formality, he was escorted to the vaults by a dignified bank official, who used his key to unlock the first of the deadbolts and then left him in privacy to complete the opening with his key. Unbuckling his back-pack he extracted the leather bags but kept a few items. One, a small modern shoulder bag, was destined to sink to the bottom of the Irish Sea, after being tossed overboard from the ferry from Scotland to Ireland. The others were easily portable coins and trinkets. They were not particularly rare and he could use these to test the market for stolen treasure trove. The rest he could retrieve gradually, as circumstances permitted and his finances dictated.

The sword he might never collect. At that moment his sense of sin was overwhelming, a throwback to his religious upbringing, which he thought he had long since rejected. Would sacrificing the sword, and the riches it could bring, atone for the death of a young girl? Even now he failed to accept responsibility. In his mind, the sword had been to blame. If it had not been in the hoard, too large to pack, he could have carried away the rest with his other gear and there would have been no need to return.

He cursed his greed. The sword was too significant a find to dispose of easily. He should have thought of that. If he tried to sell it, word would get out about this unique artefact and that would be dangerous. It was designed to be dangerous, he thought, to take lives and now it had taken another. He thought fleetingly of the lifeless body he had buried. No, he decided, he would not let it ruin his life. He would leave it where it had already lain for eight hundred years.

The decision made, he remained resolute for years, for decades, but always there was the pull to return to recover it, a pull he resisted until the news item about the archaeological project, tucked away at the bottom of a column in a learned journal. But there was another, more serious threat. Even a small-scale dig at that old site he had worked on so many years ago was perilous. Rather than wait, hoping there would be no negative outcome, he decided to take action to make sure he was involved at both the planning stage and the implementation.

He lifted his phone and dialled the Scottish number.

"Hello, Alan. A voice from the past here. I see you are planning a dig on Cumbrae..."

CUMBRAE 2005

"**Y**ou looked like a warrior princess, standing there with the sword blade pointing down, your hair backlit by the sun." Dean sat with Alice on the rocks near West Bay. The tide was in and they had to jump to reach the spot where a horseshoe pool of deep water faced outwards to the rocky island of Little Cumbrae.

Alice had not an ounce of vanity, although her imagination was fired by the picture Dean had drawn. "I know I go on about it, but women have been written out of so much history. I wonder if there were any Norse women ever on Cumbrae."

"There is one princess," Dean thought, but he was sensitive enough to keep the thought hidden at present and avoid the scorn he was sure Alice would pour on what she would describe as a mawkish remark. "Another time," he resolved. He held out his hand to help Alice up, happy when she didn't spurn it. They were due at the Ritz café in a few minutes.

It was only fitting that their final meeting took place in the Ritz cafe. Certain pairings were obvious as they sat down. Kathryn and Paul, Graziella and Markus, Susan and Tom - and yes, Alice and Dean. Matthias had left at midday to meet Elvira at Glasgow airport and begin walking the West Highland Way with the girl he planned to marry, when she had finished her nursing course in a couple of years. If Connor felt left out he gave no sign of it. He was already absorbed in the love song he was composing, confident it would appeal to a woman of his choice.

"So this is the photograph he wanted so desperately." Kathryn looked at the picture that Alice had handed her. Susan had given the original date-stamped photograph to Andrew MacGillivray as evidence of O'Flaherty's presence on the island, on a day when he had sworn that he was on the way back to Ireland. But she had made an enlarged version that they were examining eagerly.

"It's remarkable how recognisable he is after all these years. How could he live with the knowledge that he had killed a girl?"

"Some people have little or no conscience." Susan's career had given her a less idealistic view of human nature than Kathryn.

"Even if we believe his claim that it was an accident, it was still despicable." Dean had not a shred of pity for the man, who was still on the run from the police.

Many miles away, in a small bay on a Scottish sea loch, once traversed by Norsemen on a raid to subdue the Scots, an orange rigid inflatable boat rocked gently at anchor, among a small collection of other boats. None of their owners had been present when a burly man had off loaded a motor bike and vanished into the countryside. Their curiosity was only mildly aroused that the boat had joined the others moored there. It was a changing population and it was some time before the rogue boat, long reported missing by the original boat hiring firm, was identified and reclaimed by its owners. What had become of the man who had abandoned it remained a mystery.

In West Bay Montmorency stopped at a particularly ornate lamppost to lift his leg. and Tom looked up at the lantern, a coloured lampshade, where each of the four glass panes bore the Millport crest, ornamented with three scallop shells and three starfish.

"*Altiora vide ad.* We must look to higher things." His education at Rothesay Academy on Bute had included a good grounding in Latin, but well before that Miss Harris at Millport Primary School had made sure they knew and if possible lived up to the town motto. Now, after a successful career in the Merchant Navy, he lived in the sandstone villa, one of many that fringed the bay, a sign that this was an area, like Kames Bay, where the more well-to-do had their houses.

"They have never moved the provost's lamppost even though we don't have a provost now, since, oh I don't know when, regionalisation."

"I remember when all Scottish towns had their own town councils and the head was called the provost. In cities like Glasgow and Edinburgh they were called Lord Provosts, even when as sometimes happened they were women. It was the custom to put a lamppost outside their houses and move it when the next provost took over, I assume this one was left where the last provost lived."

"My father worked hard to buy this house, and for the town he lived in all his life. But it's too big for one person. Have you time for a coffee?" Tom opened the garden gate invitingly and Montmorency led the way inside.

171

HISTORICAL NOTE

Discerning people have always wanted to visit and to live on Cumbrae, from the Glaswegians who brought their families to spend their summer holidays 'doon the water,' back through the years to the Bronze Age tribes whose settlements are scattered around the island. In August 1873, while the first road was being laid around the Isle of Cumbrae, a Bronze Age burial site was uncovered and excavated.

Perhaps the first named visitor is King Haakon IV of Norway, thanks to whom Cumbrae gets a mention in a travel book of the thirteenth century when his biography records that he "lay at Cumbrae" in October 1263.

In the thirteenth century all of the western isles of Scotland were under Norwegian influence and a source of conflict between the Norwegian King, Haakon IV and the Scottish kings, Alexander II and his son Alexander III. The conflict which developed in the 1260s culminated in the battle of Largs (1263) after which Haakon and his fleet retreated to Norway via Orkney, where Haakon died later that year. His successor Magnus and the Scottish King Alexander III pursued a policy of diplomatic marriages instead of open warfare.

The contemporary sources are sagas and chronicles and one extraordinary book, *The King's Mirror,* whose internal evidence dates it from the 1260s. The author is unknown, but one credible theory is that it was written by Haakon's chaplain, an Englishman, Magister William, presumably recording the king's views with interspersions of the world and the bible from William's knowledge. The Norwegian record of the conflict was contemporary written within two years of the events, as

Haakon's son and successor Magnus almost immediately commissioned a chronicle of his father's life. There is also a chronicle of the Isle of Man which includes the activities of Haakon's ally, another King Magnus, during the 1263 expedition.

Scottish records are less full. The Melrose Chronicle contains many details of ecclesiastical events of the thirteenth century but deals with the invasion and its defeat in only a few lines, ascribing the victory to God.

There is no record of King Alexander IV being at Dundonald Castle in the days before the battle, but the castle was owned by his commander, Alexander Stewart, the High Steward of Scotland and it commanded a view of Arran, where much of Haakon's fleet was anchored before the storm, so this imaginary scene is not beyond the bounds of credibility.

Ragnhild is an imaginary character, but Haakon fathered children outside wedlock, including a daughter Cecilia, who married the King of Man, so Ragnhild's story could be credible, as a resolute woman who chooses for herself. The inscription on the sword is a genuine one, on a sword now in the British Museum, the secret of its meaning still as yet a mystery. The silver pennies minted in Alexander's reign have been found in many hoards across Europe, not just in Scotland.

HISTORICAL
CHARACTERS

Haakon Haakonson (1204-1263) Haakon IV King of Norway (1217-1263) came to the Norwegian throne in 1217 at the age of 13, reigned 46 years.

Margarete Skulasdottir (1208-1270) wife of Haakon IV King of Norway (1217-1263), formally engaged at nine, married in 1225.

Magister William, Haakon's chaplain, believed by some to be English and the author of *The King's Mirror*, a book of advice of a king to his son dating probably from the 1260s.

Christina Haakonsdottir (1234-1263), daughter of Haakon and Margarete Skuladottir, married at age of 24 to Prince Philip of Castile. His title as heir to the throne of Castile was the Infante of Castile, therefore she became known as the Infanta of Castile. She died the same year as her father, but whether the news had reached him before his own death is uncertain.

Haakon Haakonson, known as Ungi (the Young) (1232-1257) second legitimate son and eldest surviving son of Haakon IV, declared junior king in 1240, married Rikitsa Birginsdottir in 1251.

Magnus Haakonson (1238-1280) youngest son of Haakon IV, declared junior king in 1257 after the death of his brother Haakon Haakonson Ungi, King of Norway as Magnus VI (1263-1280).

Rikitsa Birgirsdottir, daughter of Birgir Magnusson, ruler of Sweden, Haakon's daughter-in-law, widow of his son Haakon

Haakonson (1232-1257).

Ogmund Krækidants, (crow dancer) one of Haakon's commanders at the Battle of Largs in 1263.

Sigvat Bodvarson, nephew of the historian Sturla Thordarson. He is recorded as accompanying the expedition and regarded as one of the sources Thordarson would have had as an eye witness to the events of the expedition.

Sturla Thordarson (1214-1284) Icelandic historian commissioned by Haakon's son Magnus to write his father's biography

MacGillivray (Gilaverian), farmer of Cumbrae, he and his son appear in the exchequer rolls of Scotland for 1263, where his son is taken as hostage for the payment of a fine of cattle due to Walter Stewart. The name is given in Latin as Gilaverian, which I have taken the liberty to translate as MacGillivray, having seen what census recorders did trying to record the name of the Gaelic speaking MacGillivrays in my own family.

Alexander IV, King of Scots (1241 -1286) became king in 1249 and was inaugurated that year at Scone. He married Margaret Plantagenet, daughter of King Henry III of England in 1251, when he was ten and she was eleven. Their daughter, Margaret (1261-1283) his only heir married, King Erik II of Norway, Haakon's grandson. She died in 1281 giving birth to a daughter, Margaret, known as the Maid of Norway. She was heir to the Scottish crown, but died in 1290 on her way to Scotland, leaving the country without a clear successor to the crown after the death of Alexander.

Alexander Stewart of Dundonald, fourth High Steward of Scotland (1214-1283), commander at the Battle of Largs, said to have gone on the seventh crusade 1248-1254).

Rudri of Kintyre played a significant part in the later stages of Haakon's campaign and is mentioned in the Norwegian account several times, where his brutality on Bute and in earlier raids on the mainland of Scotland are detailed, including the broken promise to allow the garrison of Rothesay Castle free passage after its surrender. His surname is not given but scholars have identified him as the second son of Reginald, King of the Isles. He is recorded as having made a donation to Saddell Abbey. His part in the fictional hoard of treasure in this story is pure supposition, but, given what we do know about him, his villainy is credible, as is my decision to have him meet a sticky end.

Walter Stewart, (1225/1230-1293/1294) Earl of Menteith, Sheriff of Ayr, brother to Alexander Stewart, Scots commander at the Battle of Largs. His nickname 'Bailloch' means freckled one. He may have had experience as a crusader in the 1258 seventh crusade led by Louis IX of France. His older brother, Robert, died on crusade.

GLOSSARY

aiblins, maybe, perhaps (Scots)

asgautr, double-edged Viking sword (Norse)

bodhran, framed drum (Irish)

bailloch, freckled (Gaelic)

ceilidh, party with music, song, dancing (Gaelic)

dub, muddy pool (Scots)

dreich, dull, grey, (of weather) overcast (Scots)

Feierabend, Closing time. Greeting when day's work is finished (German)

Feuerzangbowle, red wine and rum punch (German)

gang agley, go wrong (Scots)

morn's morn, tomorrow morning (Scots)

room and kitchen, small two-roomed apartment

petticoat tails, triangular biscuits

seax, small knife or dagger

schiltron, shield wall of warriors

skelp, skelpit, slap, slapped (Scots)

sonsy, good looking and healthy (Scots)

Tschüß, informal farewell greeting (German)

Uilleann, type of bagpipe played seated 'pipes of the elbow' (Irish)

Wadmal, coarse woollen cloth still made in Scandinavian countries

NORWEGIAN CAMPAIGN 1263-1264

Versions differ. This is one account

1263
July 7 Haakon sets sail from Bergen, Norway
August 2 Eclipse of sun while in Orkney
August and September
Attacks on Caithness and Argyll
Fleet sails down Western Isles
Raids on Loch Lomond and Bute
September Haakon's fleet anchors in the Firth of Clyde
Negotiations continue between Haakon and King Alexan-
der
Sunday 30 September storm begins
October 1 transport ship drifts
Royal ship is damaged
Haakon lands on Cumbrae
Some ships grounded on beach at Largs
October 2
Haakon leads force to save cargo of transport ship
Scots attack.
October 4
Norwegian bodies removed for burial, probably on Bute
Haakon moves his ship further out. Weather improves
October 5 Haakon orders the stranded ships burned
Fleet moves to Arran
Fleet departs West of Scotland to sail to Orkney
November Haakon taken ill in Orkney

December 12 Last rites administered to Haakon
December 16 Haakon's death
Burial in St Magnus' Cathedral, Orkney
1264
March Haakon's body exhumed and taken to Norway
March 21 Haakon buried in Christchurch, Bergen

RECIPES

CLOOTIE DUMPLING

Clean cotton or linen tea towel and string to tie up

250g plain flour
125g suet
Orange peel or grated rind
3 heaped teaspoon mixed spice
1 level teaspoon salt
200g currants
100g sultanas
2 level teaspoons bicarbonate of soda
Milk to mix
(Optional, a lucky silver coin in greaseproof paper)

Put flour in bowl
Add dry ingredients
Mix well with milk
Scald cloth and dust with flour
Put mixture in centre of cloth
Tie, leaving room to expand.
Boil 4 hours in large pan

COCK-A-LEEKIE SOUP

1 small chicken, or several chicken pieces
3 carrots
2 litres water
salt and pepper to season
1 tablespoon chopped parsley
25g rice
1 leek

Wash chicken and put in large pan of cold salted water
Bring to boil and simmer for 2 hours
Add chopped leek and washed rice and cook for 30 more minutes
Remove chicken and skim off fat
Add grated carrots for last ten minutes
Season to taste and garnish with parsley.

CRANACHAN

450ml double cream
1 tablespoon honey (optional)
55g oatmeal (gently toasted)
Raspberries crushed, but keep some whole to garnish
3 tablespoons malt whisky (optional)

Whisk the cream with the whisky (if used) into peaks
Fold in the oatmeal and honey
Layer cream and raspberries, finishing with cream layer
Garnish with whole raspberries and a sprinkling of oatmeal
Cover and chill for at least an hour before serving

FEUERZANGBOWLE

2 oranges, 2 lemons. 2 bottles dry red wine
1 cinnamon stick, 5 cloves, 1 pinch ground ginger
1 sugar cone
2 cups brown rum at least 54% alcohol

Wash oranges and lemons thoroughly
Pat dry and cut into slices or wedges
Add red wine, cinnamon, cloves and ginger
Heat slowly in large pot
Make sure it does not come to a boil
Remove pot from heat and place on a heatproof surface
Place sugar cone on metal holder (the "Feuerzange")
Soak sugar cone with rum and light it carefully
The sugar will melt and drip into the wine
Add more rum to sugar cone with long-handled ladle
Once the sugar and rum finished, stir gently
Serve in mugs or heatproof glasses

PETTICOAT TAILS

300g plain flour
200g butter salted or unsalted
100g caster sugar

Cream the butter and sugar
Add the flour
Bring the dough together by hand
Roll into a round shape to desired thickness
Pinch round the edge with two fingers
Cut to mark 8 slices and prick top with a fork
Chill 30 minutes in the fridge
Transfer onto a baking tray
Bake 25 minutes at a 180°c till lightly browned
Cut the marked slices again
Cool then separate into individual 'petticoats'
Sprinkle with caster sugar (optional)

POTATO SCONES

200g cooked potatoes
Butter
50g flour or oatmeal
Salt 1 level teaspoonful
Baking powder pinch

Mash potatoes while hot with butter and salt.
Add baking powder to the flour or oatmeal.
Work flour/oatmeal into potatoes to make a dough.
Roll out very thinly.
Cut into four or six scones, fork.
Cook on hot griddle for 3 minutes each side.
Serve hot or cold, buttered.

ABOUT THE AUTHOR

Margaret MacGregor lives on the west coast of Scotland, within sight of the island of Arran and, on a good day, the Isle of Cumbrae and the Mull of Kintyre. She studied Scottish and medieval history at the University of Glasgow in the 1960s.

Cover Page - Viking Ship Sculpture, Largs
original image copyright Margaret MacGregor
Paperback back page - Crocodile Rock
original image copyright Margaret MacGregor

The cover page image features a stainless steel sculpture, by Giusseppe Lund, which was commissioned in 1996 by Largs Marina to mark the site of the last Viking invasion of Scotland and the Battle of Largs in 1263. It was inspired by the lines of a Viking longboat, the head and detailing paying homage to Nordic mythology and symbolism. Originally it was fixed to the breakwater of large rocks so that waves could wash against it in rough weather and is now sited above this spot.

The paperback back page image is of the iconic crocodile rock, a natural feature in the town of Millport on the Isle of Cumbrae, Scotland.

ACKNOWLEDGEMENT

My thanks to Tatjana Schmitz-Valkenberg for her enthusiastic encouragement in the initial stages, which meant the story survived, James Davidson, model-maker extraordinaire, for his knowledge of longship design and construction, Walter Kerr, whose photography in Millport over decades captured precious moments for so many families, the many shopkeepers and residents of Millport who made, and still make, the island such a friendly place for summer visitors, the late George Cosmo Douglas (1888-1973), Dean of Argyll and the Isles, for welcoming young people from Glasgow to stay at the College of the Cathedral of the Isles back in the 1960s, Gordon Hepburn for his Latin translations, Bernd Halstenberg for technical advice about motorbikes and an offer to be the stuntman when this story is made into a film, Carol Johnston, Alison Spence, Joan Davidson and Liz Hepburn for their advice on draft versions and Rae Gold for her help in turning my photograph into a book cover, and the Gutenberg Project for its mission to make available free the writings of past ages, where I first found and read the Norse account of Haakon's 1263 expedition, which inspired this story.

Reviews can be left in the usual way. Comments can also be sent to belnahuabooks@gmail.com